The Steamy Adventures of the

Goddesses

From

Atlantis

By Kelly Comans

This story is dedicated to the first author known to human history. Not only was she a woman (and a woman of color at that!), but also the high priestess of Nanna/Inanna, the Sumerian god/goddess of sex and transgender people, moreover, she wrote erotica about the gods and goddesses of her people.

So, when the critics critic and the haters hate, all because this fantasy—written by a woman—is sexually driven, body positive, and transwoman inclusive, let us remember that so were the first stories ever written down, and so was the world's first author.

Here's to you, Enheduanna.

And, also, here's to what I'm positive will surmount to my first book to hit the ban lists!

C.S. KELLY

Acknowledgements:

A special thank you to The Book Well Agency and my editors, K. Boutwell and S. Shaw, as well as their fantastic design team, and K Boutwell of the USA, who came together to create such beautiful "safe-for-work" and "not-safe-for-work" covers for "The Steamy Adventures of the Goddesses from Atlantis".

In addition, I would like to express my heartfelt gratitude to the following individuals for their contributions to research for this story: C.S.Kelly, K. Boutwell, and D. C. Boutwell.

And, a special thank you to the TikTok communities of BookTok, Authortok, and Smuttok for inspiring me to make the terrifying leap from "Closed-Door" Romance author to writing and releasing such *Spicy* stories and characters. Thank you to such authors as Elle M. Drew and Charlie Nottingham for inspiring me to write the romance heroines I have always wanted to read: strong, saucy, curvy, and confident!

And, of course, a word of thanks to my alpha readers, sensitivity readers, beta readers, and ARC readers. Also, to my spouse, daughter, pets, family, friends, and TikTok followers, because y'all keep me motivated!

I could fill an entire book with nothing but gratitude; but, for conciseness's sake, I will keep it short and sweet and to just one page:

THANK YOU!

C. S. Kelly

The Book Well
LITERARY AGENT, EDITOR, AND COACH

The Steamy Adventures of the Goddesses From Atlantis

By Kelly Comans

Chapter One: The Future Queen of Atlantis

Princess Aegaea D'Lumeria

"And," my mother—the venerated Siren Queen Thelxeipiea D'Lumeria III, current reigning monarch of Atlantis—concludes her two-hour-long, tedious public address, facing the cameras and dozens of members of the press just a few paces before us.

I am bored beyond comprehension as she informs our public of mundane details of the nation's state of affairs. All details I am intimately familiar with, since my she and my grandmothers drill the information into my head every morning before my hours-long tutoring sessions.

"As a final note, I wish to address the obvious. I am not as spry of fin as I once was..."

My head moves only slightly as I eye her from the corner of my vision. I know I am not to look away from the camera in an official address, such as this; as princess, I am to silently sit next to my mother in solidarity. However, I cannot help myself as she springs this unanticipated announcement upon me.

"What is she doing...?!" I wonder. *"Where is she going with this...? Surely, she's not...?"*

I glance to her wife, the Queen Consort, to her left. The woman who has been my second parent since birth, a mermaid named Hyraeth. She, too, spares a suspicious glance to her other half.

Mother refuses to meet either of our glances. Instead, she continues after a brief pause, "It is time our *great* kingdom begins looking toward the future," She continues, "Recently, I have been approached by my daughter's mentors and advisors and I am exceedingly proud to announce they have informed me that she has completed her studies much sooner than expected—at a younger age, in fact, than any of her foremothers. She has surpassed all markers for completion of the Royal Curriculum; and, as such, I see no reason she should be forced to wait for her crown any longer than necessary. As many of you will remember, I was much older than she when I completed my studies and, consequentially, I am nearing the end of my prime. I grow weary. I am ready to pass on my crown and the responsibility of ruling Atlantis. However, as you all know, to be eligible to receive the crown, she must complete the most sacred task and obligation of being born to the Crown of Lumeria..."

A hush of whispers spreads through the press before us; though, the members of my mothers' council all smile down at me, wrinkled faces full of wisdom and pride, from their perches on the raised benches to our left and right.

Mother continues her public address, "Aegaea shall travel to the surface world," The queen informs the entire nation, and me, "To perform the Sacred Rite. For," her eyes cut to me and our gazes meet, "Whom but a mother can be a queen? Only mothers have the wisdom, love, and patience required to adequately carry out the role. For the sake of Atlantis, Aegaea must mate a human male and produce the next heir, before she may take the throne. These are our traditions, and I shall see them honored and upheld. For Atlantis."

In every home in Atlantis, I know millions of selks and mermaids and a few hundred sylphs will currently be repeating, "For Atlantis."

But what sacrifice are any of *them* making '*for Atlantis*'? I don't see any of *them* heading up *there,* to the world we are warned about and taught to fear and loathe from the time we are little merlings and selklings and sylphlings. I don't see any of them *fucking* disgusting, unintelligent humans for the sake of procreation and saving our species… I don't see any of them going through the pain of childbirth—all for the love of Atlantis.

Atlantis has to have a siren—a mermaid of one particular lineage, blessed by Calliope with magical song— on the throne; and, since no mermen have existed in nearly twelve generations, and neither selkies and mermaids nor sylphs and mermaids can reproduce together, there's only one way I can produce an heir: I must trick a human male into impregnating me.

"Fuck."

"No one will come looking for us… at least for a moment, anyway," I whisper as I pull my most 'extra-*special'* armed guard into a small lavatory I'm quite familiar with and lock the door behind us. "I can't allow Mother to send me to the surface without a proper farewell, now can I?"

I cannot suppress the hysterical, panicked giggle that escapes my throat as I press myself against her, running my hands across her firm, furry, sea-otter-like chest.

"You know," I murmur, still processing my mother's announcement, "I think I'm going to miss you while I'm up there, Commander Lochlynn..."

"Surely not, Your Highness," she denies me verbally, but not physically, her emerald green eyes glittering brilliantly in the plasmatic lighting inside the Palace of Lumeria and all of Atlantis, "There are many just like me in the sea," she says, as she often does, "Besides, you shall have your way with and be satisfied by all the human men you could possibly desire..."

"Humans, bleh," I roll my eyes, "And *men*. So *boring*! I've always had a...*fondness* for women, you know... *Particularly*, selkie women..."

"Ah," she giggles, "I've come to suspect that."

I grab her by her thick, mattlocked blonde hair at the back of her skull and I yank her downward, until her mouth and mine collide. My hands grasp at her thick thighs—her neck, her shoulders, biceps, breasts... All delicious!

I pull my mouth from her nipples to kiss her neck, dragging my tongue between her smooth, soft breasts, kissing down her abs, forcing a soft whimper and moan from her throat.

Selk guards are bare from the waist up—aside from their animal furs and weapons often worn strapped to their bodies—as a large fraction of their profession includes being servants to my mother's personal pleasure... and, more recently, mine as well.

Lochlynn is quite young to have achieved her position; but, we have a long and intimate history and she has all the qualities I find *most* attractive in my Head of Security, as well as a romantic partner: ambition, skill, and loyalty.

Her thick, curvy, sculpted physique, gorgeous eyes, and respectful hands didn't hurt, either...

"Although, in moments such as these, the respectful hesitation of her hands can be quite frustrating..."

I grab hold of both her wrists and I place her hands upon my breasts. They cannot contain the glorious mountains; but, they try their best as Lochlynn finally loses control and abandons restraint.

She captures my mouth with hers once more and her tongue pries between my lips.

I run mine along hers, tasting her sweet, salty flavor. My hands clutch her face to mine.

One of her hands relinquishes my breast and dives below, slipping inside the slick slit hidden among my glimmering golden scales.

Within just a moment, she has found her treasure and she caresses my pearl between her middle and index fingers, moving them back and forth.

A moan escapes my parted lips as she pulls her mouth from mine.

I drift backward, propelled by the involuntary spasms in my fins, pulling her with me, until I reach the washing basin. I lift myself and carefully perch upon the edge.

Eagerly, she dives tongue-deep into my slit.

I gasp as her hot, slick tongue parts my lips, lapping and flicking. She uses her upper lip to rub my clit as her tongue plunges in and out of me. I grab the back of her head and pull her into me, harder.

Her lips pucker and kiss my pleasure-button, delicately at first but with building intensity, sucking and nibbling until I am gasping loudly, grabbing at the edge of the wash basin beneath me, squirming back, into the mirror that reflects our explicit scene.

I can feel my juices sliding out, my pussy begging for her. She's not used to not getting what she wants, when she wants it...

Instinctively knowing what I need, Lochlynn begins caressing my hole with her index and middle finger, slowly moving in circles around the outer edges.

I tremble and jerk, fighting the urge to beg...

Just as I am about to forget my pride and do exactly that, she plunges both fingers inside me, twisting and spreading them, pulling them back out and shoving them back in. All the while, her tongue flicks my clit with surprising, *shocking* speed and strength.

Within seconds, I am moaning and writhing, bucking and grinding against her hand and face.

My hands find my breasts and they squeeze and caress them, pulling and pushing, pinching my own nipples...

"Fuck, I LOVE breasts," I think, barely able to form thoughts, *"Especially mine."*

Lochlynn adds a third finger and I cry out in pleasure. I grab her head once again and hold her to me, grinding on her face as shock wave after shock wave of orgasm washes over me.

I'm not finished, though; one is never enough to satisfy me.

I shove her away from me, playfully, and she lands on her ass on the bathroom floor. I drop to the floor with her and begin yanking off her fur.

Beneath her standard-issue military weapons—and the removal, magic pelt she was born with—I find a pair of underwear barely more than string anywhere but the front, which is a large triangle of black leather. I am both impressed and excited by them.

I release a feral snarl-slash-moan as I rip them down her legs, as well.

She titters anxiously, anticipating what she knows from previous experience is to come…

For a fraction of a moment, I take in my *most* favorite conquest, laying naked on the floor in front of me.

"Life is so, soo good," I think as I crawl across the floor and up her body.

I lift her leg and lick from behind her knee—softly, slowly—down her soft, smooth thigh. Legs do prove to be a complicating factor when pleasuring a selkie, sylph, or—*ugh, I might as well get used to the idea*—humans; but, I've found Lochlynn's pale, thick, muscular legs particularly alluring and mysterious, since early puberty as a young Merling, fascinated by *all* bodies, years and years ago….

"Not that it's much different, now that I am grown," I think, *"Quite the opposite..."*

The sweet scent of her womanhood in the waters around me elicits a warm flow of my own nectars, dispersing into the water around us, mixing with hers.

She moans, her eyes rolling back in her head slightly. Her fingers slide across the slick, polished stone floors, searching for purchase and finding none.

I nibble at the crease where her round, ample buttock meets the plain of her inner thigh, following the crevice with my tongue.

Lochlynn gasps, inhaling loudly, as my tongue reaches the intersection of creases just below her treasure trove... Then, with little warning, I plunge into her depths, lapping every deliciously salty-sweet drop from her folds.

I am sure to explore her as deeply as my well-practiced tongue can reach, darting in and out, teasingly.

Lochlynn bucks her hips upward, begging for more—*deeper*—and pants loudly.

I fold my slippery, webbed fingers together to form a shell-like shape. Withdrawing my tongue from her crevasse and slowly licking her clit with the flat, warm top of it, I slowly—*desperately slowly*—begin to press my fingertips into her, twisting slowly at my wrist to help guide my hand in past the third knuckles.

Lochlynn moans, her eyes squeezed shut and her mouth forming a perfect rose-tinted 'O'. "*Ohhhhh,*" she breathes, overwhelmed and unsure she'll be able to fit it all…

While I continue to slowly, gently, deeply lap at her clit, I also gently stretch her inner lip with my thumb—only rubbing the tight ring at first, then opening my hand up a bit inside her and slipping it in where my folded hand and fingers create a tiny opening.

"*Ah!!!*" She cries out, her eyes flying open.

I read her body and expression and sounds, and the rhythms and pulses of her body and I *know...*

I flick my tongue with frantic *need,* pressing my face—nose and all; who needs to breathe?—into her sweet-smelling slit. My mouth desperately works to elicit the elixir of the goddess I'm so hopelessly addicted to.

Meanwhile, I push my fist into her further, until my entire wrist disappears.

She pants, her eyes wide and rolling back, her mouth open as she gasps for breath. She grabs my head, pulling me deeper into her soft flesh.

I circle her clit with the tip of my tongue—round and round and round—then, I *FLICKFLICKFLICKFLICKFLICK!* As fast and hard as I can manage.

I pull out of her, slowly, until my wrist, thumb, hand, and finally my fingers reappear, almost to the nails. Then, I slam back into her.

Again.

In, *ooouuut,* In!

Out! IN! OUT!

IN!

OUT!

In, Out, In, Out!

I pump my arm harder and faster as my tongue practically vibrates.

With another upward thrust of her hips, Lochlynn cums in my mouth, spraying my face and arm with her potent, salty-sweet juices.

"Ugh!" she groans as she rocks back and forth on my face, milking my tongue for every spasm of ecstasy it bring her.

I free my hand from her vice grip and gently lick her clean of our mess as she whimpers and giggles and begs me to stop, overwhelmed and overstimulated in the *best* possible way.

Once I am satisfied with my accomplishment, I slip across the floor, propelled by my golden-scaled fin, until I am able to cuddle up in her arms.

For several minutes, we lay just like that, breathless and shameless in our ecstasy.

Once I am able, I pull myself up off the cold, hard floor.

"Who's your Queen?" I ask, tauntingly, a grin playing at my lips as I dangle Lochlynn's tiny undergarments from a fingertip, just out of her reach. "C'mon, say my name..."

She grins back, thoroughly enjoying my game, "I, Lochlynn Orca-Chaser, eternally serve the Crowned *Princess* of Atlantis, one devilishly devious Aegaea D'Lumeria."

As she clambers to her feet, she snatches the leather from my fingers and plants a kiss upon my brow.

"Atta Girl," I praise her, knowing she has a special reaction to such words, "Say it again, lest you forget."

"I serve my future queen, Princess Aegaea D'Lumeria." She repeats, "Until my dying breath." She leans in for one more kiss.

It's unprofessional and inappropriate, but I allow it. It might be the last we get, after all...

While the kingdom sleeps, I sneak—alone—to the outer rim.

Like a trapped bubble, the protective dome of Atlantis sits at the bottom of the ocean, so far beneath the surface that light does not reach. We make our own.

I reach my hand out and place it against the wall of energy. It's pleasantly cold. It ripples beneath my fingertips.

This completely natural forcefield keeps us safe—from the harsh environment, from sharks and other predators, from enemies of our people… from *humans*.

Atlantis is so *ethereally* beautiful; how can I bear to leave even for a few months to live on the surface, where I know the humans have completely destroyed Mother Earth's natural beauty? Where they've built grotesque structures and leached all life from her soils? Where they've polluted our planet's land, just as they've tried so hard to pollute and kill her oceans.

If not for us, Earth and all who dwell upon her would have died centuries ago...

How can Mother expect me—*me! Her perfect, precious princess!*—to survive even a day up there?! Much less *months*?!

Three whole months away from my beloved sea, my beloved Atlantis, my beloved family... my beloved Lochlynn?

The thought springs tears to my eyes.

Just outside the dome, I can see two sea lions frolicking.

The selks worship and tend them. As a result, they expect food when so near the edge of the dome.

I oblige and offer a small square of fish from my evening meal, brought specifically for them.

They come right to the edge and snatch the fish away with their teeth as soon as I extend it past the energy-wall, into the waters of The Wilds.

"I thought I'd find you here," a soft, musical voice behind me turns my head and I see Lochlynn swimming toward me. "What's the meaning of you sneaking off, in the dead of night?"

She wears her magic fur, allowing her to transform between an appearance indistinguishable from a mortal human to one impossible to differentiate from a normal sea otter, or any state between. Presently, she appears as her striking woman-like self from the chest up; from her ribs down her elongated lower two-thirds, she takes her furry otter form, which propels her swiftly through the water with webbed flipper-feet and navigational tail.

"Do you remember the first time we ever snuck out, into The Wilds?" I ask, turning my attention back to the dome's barrier. "We were—what?—ten? Eleven?"

"Ten, I think," she answers, just behind my shoulder now, "I think that was one of the only times my father ever truly *yelled* at me... but, he had to travel regularly for work, didn't he? He *knew* what's out there... how dangerous it can be beyond the wall..."

Lochlynn's father was an Atlantian diplomat to the Selk clans who eek a perilous, survivalist existence out of The Wilds. He met his own devastating fate just beyond the dome, only a year or so after that, to a shark.

"We were fearless," I comment, peering out, into the dark unknown, "I wish I could feel like that right now..."

"You're afraid?" Lochlynn whispers, and I can feel her penetrative gaze on the side of my face. "Of the open sea? You never were before, when we were little girls..."

"It's different, now, isn't it?" I whisper back, lifting my hand to place my palm against the energetic forcefield. It is warm and humming beneath my skin but does not hurt or damage me in any way. Sharks and most other sea life refuse to cross it, though. It disrupts several of their internal organs and senses. "We *know* the danger... which, in some strange way, is also comforting. But, when it comes to the surface world, we know so little... Humans are said to be far more dangerous than a shark or orca or giant octopus."

"You have nothing to fear, My Queen," Lochlynn's voice is stiff and formal, as though she fears being overheard, "I'll be there to protect you, through every second."

"What?" I feel as though my insides turn to stone, "No! It's too dangerous! If you—"

"*Exactly,*" she insists, shedding her armor of stoic professionalism, and floating closer, "It's *dangerous.* Am I your Head of Security, or was my promotion last month just some nepotistic charity case? What would everyone think if I *didn't* go with you to keep you safe? But, public opinion aside, what would *I* think of myself if I let you go alone? How could I live with myself if something awful happened? I took an oath to protect you with my life, remember? And," she pauses, glancing down at my lips then back up, into my eyes, "my life would be naught without you."

I grab her, wrapping my hand around the nook where her jaw meets her neck, and I pull her in for a deep, passionate kiss.

Her hand slips inside the gold-plated, shell-shaped armor fitted around my breasts and cups my right boob. Her fingers caress and gently pinch my rock-hard nipple.

The chilly waters out here close to the wall have made my metal chest-piece like ice. Generally, pieces such as these are worn by mermaids and sirens *over* other garments, insulating 'the girls' from the metal.

I prefer the sensation of the cold metal against my delicate nips.

I spin slightly in her arms until we are chest-to-chest, and I grab a handful of her amble, exposed breast. Bare to the icy waters, she, too, is pert and erect.

I duck my head and suck one of her nipples into my mouth, nibbling and flicking it with my tongue in rhythm with my fingers playing with its sister.

"Mmmm," she moans, tilting her head back and closing her eyes.

My free hand dives below.

Her deep, ragged breathing hitches just slightly as I slide my longest finger beyond her fur, into her slick, slippery opening.

Chapter Two:
Selkie Security Services

Locklynn Orca-Chaser

Aegaea's webbed fingers expertly locate and play at the opening hidden in my thick, reddish-brown pelt. The fingers are as familiar with my body as her own and do not stray or fumble as they locate and massage my clitoris, just inside the fleshy folds and fur.

My breath comes in uncontrollable bursts and explosions. My body transforms water to air—part of the ancient, mystical magic gifted to our foremothers and forefathers by our goddess, Rán—and bubbles appear from my mouth and rising up, up, up, and disappear far beyond the dome.

Aegaea's other hand releases my breast and joins its partner, slipping between my nether-lips and entering me with no hesitation... like a person swimming through the door of their own home...

It's just three fingers at first, but I know that won't satisfy her *need* to fill me to capacity...

Aegaea pumps those three fingers in and out of my slick hole, all while the fingers of her other hand flick and twiddle the delicate bundle of nerves just above.

Her mouth abandons my titty and now-stinging nips—they bounce buoyantly in the rippled wake of her movements below—and travels down my abs, licking the thin stretch of human-like skin that reaches nearly to my navel, tracing the contours of my muscles.

Eventually, she makes the leap. Her mouth jumps from the strip of bare skin, down to my fun-zone.

I drift backward, allowing myself to float on my back as a true otter would on the surface, lazing away...

Aegaea is pulled along, refusing to release her prey, floating with me.

Her face parts the fur and flesh and her tongue laps at the skinfolds that hide my clit.

She gives a good hard kick of her golden fin and suddenly she's turned around on me entirely! In an impressive work of acrobatics, she presents her gleaming, flushed, very-aroused pussy just a finger's-length from my face.

I might be taken by surprise, but I do not hesitate for a moment before diving into my indulgence...

And, neither does my partner.

"*Ughh!*" I cry out as Aegaea plunges her entire fist into me.

I feel her snicker as she continues to lap away with furious intensity at my clit.

I can feel a deep, growing, glowing warm starting at my flipper-toes and filling me up.

One of my hands grabs my own breast, squeezing it to an almost painful extreme; the other locks its fingers in her thick, soft, abundant ringlets and pulls her face closer, her tongue deeper...

Her fist pounds at my cervix, punching it in the most pleasurably painful way... beating it into submission, demanding it relinquish her bounty: an orgasm.

I fight it.

I don't want it to be over, yet. I know this is all a distraction. I know she doesn't want to talk about me coming with her to the surface.

Which... is fine.

Because it's not up for discussion.

I'm coming.

"I'm coming," I say, firmly, "To the surface... with you," I clarify, breathlessly, "I can't... let you go... without me. It's not... even... just about... safety... Gae... *Oh, ooooh,*" I lose my train of thought for a second as I nearly topple off that cliff into the vast sea of ecstasy. I catch myself, though, and push back the wave of pleasure threatening to knock me over, "*Mmmmmmm,*" I struggle to remember where I was going with that particular thought. "I-I-I... *Oh, fuck*! I want... to *be there*..." I try to explain, "I... I... I love you. I want to be there... when... it happens... when... you... do it..."

Her tongue slows, though she continues to pull her hand, wrist, and first third of her forearm out of me and ram it back in so hard that it knocks the breath from my lungs every few words.

She seems to be considering my request.

"Pl-please," I stutter as figurative wave after wave threatens to take me under. I can feel the walls of my pussy quivering, begging for release... "I... I want... *to come!"*

"M-tay," She mumbles with her tongue still stuck out of her mouth, lapping my juices and flicking my little pebble. She shrugs lightly, then resumes her steady, quick, powerful rhythm pounding my insides, *"Tom!"*

Triumph and relief wash over me, swept away by the tidal wave of pleasure and euphoria as I obey my Queen's demand.

Chapter Three:
A Strange New World

Aegaea

Just three days later, I have packed two foreign-looking bags with the foreign-looking human clothes provided by my mother, as well as my most-prized, most-life-sustaining items: a shell necklace gifted to me by my great-grandmother, my golden gauntlets, my crown… all things I am sure I cannot live without but cannot wear once on the surface, lest I draw the humans' attention to myself. All things I often simply must look upon or touch to feel comfort and control.

Lochlynn won our dispute (a rarity and proof I never really *wanted* to leave her behind) and stands at my left, a bag of her own in hand, just as strange and otherworldly as my own.

We each take a deep breath of clean, unpolluted Atlantian water—our last for a while—before loading into the Pod, the transparent, orb-shaped, bubble-like vessel which is to carry us to the surface.

Inside, we are greeted by two familiar faces: Yandra, a mermaid, and selk Orvius Eel-Wrangler, my mother's most trusted liaisons and ambassadors to the surface world and the few selks and sylphs who choose to live amongst the humans. Both express gratitude for being chosen for and trusted with this most vital mission and swear oaths to see us returned safely.

Safely and pregnant.

My heart races as our Pod rises toward the crest of the dome, then passes through it as though it were not there at all, rising still toward the sun.

We travel across the ocean, through the gulf, and pass through the mouth of the Mississippi River. The water grows murky and visibility diminishes to next to nothing.

Orvius floats us just below the glittering surface and extends a scope camouflaged to resemble the skull and eyes of an alligator.

Slowly, like the lurking, stalking, prowl of the creature we mimic, we make our way up the river, past barges and riverboats and speedboats and bass boats, underneath bridges that seem to stretch from horizon to horizon, through bayous and past deltas—all bowing down to the river like faithful denizens to a Goddess Queen.

Yanda informs us of our destination, as we draw near. "It is nothing like anything you've ever seen or experienced," she warns us, "Dirty. Gritty. Human. It is the city that dances all day and night right at the Mississippi's edge, daring her to drag the entire town to her muddy bed by the light of sunrise. The air always smells of spirits and beer, barbeque and seafood, cigarettes and vomit, pop-corn and funnel cake, and something oddly floral. The city that sings and *oozes* music like puss from a wound."

She speaks with a level of reverence I've only ever heard used when speaking of Atlantis or—more specifically—the spectacular palace of

Lumeria and her surrounding grounds...

When she speaks the city's name, it is with the same love and devotion as a mother speaking her daughter's name aloud for the first time, or an artist naming her masterpiece:

"New Orleans."

The stealth systems of the high-tech transluscent orb make it nearly invisible; however, for extra security to remain undiscovered by the humans, we wait until the cover of nightfall to bring the Pod in to shore.

Orvius navigates us into a secluded bayou several miles from the furthest reaches of the city named New Orleans, and bogs down our Orb in a hopeless slurry of muck and maze of cypresses.

"You claim the humans will actually come and fetch us, if we simply beacon them with... *this*?" I interrogate him, finding it hard to believe his promises. I am holding a small, rectangular, black device he calls a '*cellphone*'. Supposedly, it contains a system he calls the '*internet*' and '*apps*'. It all sounds very similar to the information-exchange system Atlantis employees for various professions (though designed initially for the medical profession) which we refer to as *The Bubble.* Strange, though, that the device would store the humans' version of *The Bubble,* rather than their brains... how unhandy it must be. What if one were to lie the thing down and lose it? "And transport us to the city you call *New Orleans*?"

Orvius and Yandra both chortle and nod. Orvius reclaims his device from my outstretched palm, "We must pay them, of course," he explains, "The humans do not do anything unless they receive money for it, or pay money to do it."

"They have very strange systems," Yandra clarifies, "It will take some getting used to. Just remember: *never* take anything without asking the humans who much it cost and paying the money. Orvius and I will assist with this—one of the numerous reasons for our next rule: *never* leave your suite without Orvius or I to accompany you. This is for your safety, of course, Your Highness." She stares me down from the other side of the Pod.

"And, lastly," Orvius continues for her, "Rule number three: no getting too familiar with the humans. We are aware that the nature of your mission dictates a certain amount of... *fraternization*, in order to seduce the human males. *However*, remember to use your aliases and *never* reveal your true names or *any* information about yourselves or Atlantis."

I just blink at him. What kind of fool do they think we are? *I* am? I'm the Crowned Princess, completely trained to rule the nation he is warning me not to run my silly little girl mouth about... It's infuriating.

"I think that one goes unsaid," Yandra smirks at me, reading my face. She reaches across the Pod, to her left, and pats her mate's knee, "The Princess and her Head of Security know better than to have loose lips.

Forgive him, Your Highness, it's typically more common folk we ferry to the surface and help assimilate. And, typically, they plan to be amongst the humans for a far briefer stay—on holiday, mostly. Occasionally, we oversee other ambassadors and legal professionals, as well as students planning to study humans in the field... It's not every day that royalty travels to the surface..."

"Once in a generation," I say, feeling incredibly lonely. The world my mother visited, once, would not exist today; the world of the humans is always changing, always evolving, growing, getting closer and closer to catching up with us...

"Once in a career, to be sure," Orvius adds, oblivious to my melancholy.

"Well," I feel numb, detached from my body and reality, "I plan to accomplish my mission as swiftly as possible and return home. Hopefully, this will all be behind us soon and you'll be left with a story to brag to your grandkids about, one day: the story of how you aided the birth of their next queen."

Orvius looks as though he's about to cream his pants from the ego exploding out of every orifice, too large to be contained in his walrus-selk body. He wears his personal pelt around his waist, the tusks bound together and covering his genitals, hiding them from view. His face is red, his whiskers trembling with bottled-up excitement.

With the Pod docked, we gather our luggage and prepare to disembark, stepping foot for the first time in either mine or Lochlynn's lifetimes upon surface earth.

I watch as Orvius reaches across the Pod and places his hand on Yandra's orange-and-white fin. Before my eyes, it begins to morph and separate, into two human legs.

From my periphery, I can see Lochlynn take a deep breath and reach for my flipper in much the same way. I can feel her light, cool touch as she places her palm against my golden scales.

I'm almost scared to watch... Like when you go to the infirmary as a child and the medical technician has to perform some slightly-painful procedure. I don't have time to look away, though, before my bottom half begins to mutate and transform. Within moments, two thick, chunky, legs with dimply knees replace my once-glorious, shimmering, glimmering, golden flipper.

Almost immediately, the dissociation I'm already experiencing has multiplied until it reaches new dysphoric heights.

I love my body.

Like, I *really* love my body. Almost as much as I love Lochlynn's body. I love to look at it, touch it, play with it... I enjoy running my hands over my scales and my curves... but, somehow, that confidence is suddenly shattered.

My glitter is gone...

I blink back tears as I look up to see Lochlynn transforming into her most-human-like self. Her otter pelt is worn like a micro-dress to cover her prettiest parts.

Learning to operate my new human-legs takes some getting used to. We seem to practice walking farther than I'd travel swimming from the wall of the dome to the city of Atlantis and back!

A few hours later, Orvius seems to finally be satisfied with my clumsy excuse for walking just enough to call us an '*Uber*'—a human in a human-Pod who will come fetch us and transport us to the city.

"If the human asks what is wrong with you or why you cannot walk very well," Yandra instructs me while Orvius fiddles with his '*cellphone*', "Just say you drank too much. Everyone in New Orleans does this; he will think nothing of it. You will see for yourself, soon enough," she warns me with a coy grin, "when we get there."

"What do you mean?" I ask as I hear a strange sound approaching and glance up to see what sort of creature could possibly be creating it. My heart races, fearing the worst. “What’s that sound?” I hiss to her, “Is it some land beast?”

Yandra snickers and shakes her head, “It’s the human version of a Pod. Some of them make quite a lot of noise. That’ll be our *Uber*. Remember: you’re a tourist and you drank too much.”

“I’m a tourist and I drank too much,” I repeat after her, though the words mean little more to me than their literal translations.

The most outlandish, vaguely animal-shaped monstrosity comes around a corner in the overgrowth and trees and approaches our small party, following a strip of earth that is comprised of hard, rough, gray stone. It bounces and creaks painfully as it dips into a few craters in its path. It slows gradually until it is directly before us, where it stops.

There are transparent rectangles surrounding the upper portion (though the human technology does not seem to be quite as efficient as ours at achieving complete translucence) and within the vessel I see my first human, ever.

His skin is much darker than my own, which is the darkest in our party, tand his head is completely devoid of hair. His face is shaped quite like that of a newborn narwhal, soft and pudgy, with nearly no nose.

The human reaches down and does something below our sightline and the transparent panel next to him lowers and disappears into the white metal below. "Uber?" He inquires.

"That's us," Orvius nods, reaching out and taking hold of a spot notched into the metal. He pulls it and a door opens along undisguised fault-lines. Did humans not have to deal with intelligent predators like our sharks, orcas, giant octopuses, and such, attempting to break into their vessels to make easy meals of them? An octopus would make quick work of wriggling its tentacles into those cracks... an orca or a shark would know exactly where to slam its deadly-powerful blow to snap the doors *right* open... *'but, I guess there aren't any octopuses or sharks or orcas up here, are there?'*

I attempt to hide my trepidation as I squeeze into the small vessel, along with my three companions, and the human operator *wheels* us off.

There are four wheels on the bottom of the vessel, where legs and feet would be located on most land-walking creatures, like alligators and otters, and they roll the vessel along paths of hardened earth where no trees or foliage sprout. Also, there is another wheel, which the human holds in his lap and turns periodically, in what seems to be a method to control the direction of our vessel's travel.

'Fascinating…'

"Are these things difficult to operate?" I whisper to Yandra, "I'd very much like to attempt to pilot one while I am here…" I've always had a fondness for piloting Pods back home, especially a small one-occupancy one I'd been given for my last birthday… And, before I'd learned to pilot Pods, since childhood, in fact, I've had a passion for dolphin riding. Mother even brought in an esteemed instructor for me and a famous trainer for my dolphins.

There's something about speed that I simply cannot get enough of... and—I'm only going on a hunch here—I have a feeling this thing can travel much faster than our human driver cares to go. I shall be sorely disappointed, if I am wrong...

The human glances back at me in a tiny mirror above his head. The movement of his eyes catches my attention, "What? My car? It's just a Toyota, Lady. Automatic. Drives like any other car..."

He looks perplexed by my curiosity and I mentally vow not to inquire about anything—anything at *all*—else again until we are sequestered away to whatever private '*suite*' we have been promised for the duration of our stay. I mean, it seemed like a logical enough request to me, but I guess all humans are familiar with these vessels called '*Toyota Cars*'...

"Oh, um," I glance from the corner of my eye at Orvius, facing away from Yandra, Lochlynn, and I in the seat next to the human, "My sincerest apologies. I'm a tourist, and I've drank too much."

New Orleans is everything Yandra promised and more. The city is like one massive school of tiny fish—except, the fish are all humans and they are not so coordinated. Too many to ever truly see the individuals, though; like a defense mechanism against some non-existent predator.

The human architecture is strange and foreign to Lochlynn and I, nothing like the structures of Atlantis built to mimic the coral, oceanic rock formations, and other natural phenomena surrounding the city but on a much, much larger scale.

Lochlynn's emerald eyes bulge as she cranes her neck and looks up, up, up, to attempt to take in the enormous, metal-and-glass structure before us.

"The domiciles are so..."

"Angular..." I finish her sentence. "I suppose they do not have currents to contend with..."

"They do have particularly strong weather patterns—hurricanes often make it this far and further inland—and the winds and torrential rain can be quite perilous," Yandra tells us, "I've yet to understand how these buildings aren't toppled over... It's a wonder of their primitive technology, truly..." With a nod of her head she gestures us toward a set of transparent doors that open and close automatically as several humans come and go while we stand there, stunned and overcome.

Our new luggage in tow, Lochlynn and I stride confidently—both masking deep feelings of otherness and imposter syndrome with impeccable masks of bravado—through the translucent entrance and find ourselves surrounded by luxury. Crystal chandeliers and sparkling lights, gleaming gold fixtures and a small pool of water fed by a large waterfall with a mysterious source.

Plush furnishings positioned in clusters to encourage socialization.

The entire open vestibule twinkle—more so, even, than the royal ballrooms of Lumeria Palace.

"What *is* this place?" I ask Yandra in a barely-audible whisper as Orvius approaches two humans behind a gleaming black desk.

"It is a 'hotel'," she tells us, "One of the most luxurious in the city, at that... It's a place with hundreds of rooms available for travelers to stay in while visiting New Orleans—for a *hefty* price, to be sure." She explains further, upon seeing our blank expressions, "No expense or extravagance has been spared in your stay. You shall make memories to last a lifetime in your '*Coming-of-Age Outing*', Your Highness."

'*Well,*' I think, '*At least that sounds promising...*'

"Now I've gotten *that* business squared away," Orvius returns to us, tucking a small black and gold square of plastic back into the sewn-in pouch of his human clothing—a black outer piece over a white garment with round, metal wheels down the front that loop through holes and secure the garment closed over his burly, hairy chest—and patting the pouch for some reason, “Let’s get you up to your suite, Princess Aegaea. You can get settled in while we await sundown.”

“What happens at sundown?” I inquire as Orvius and Yandra steer Lochlynn and I in a direction that seems to have no particular significance to me.

“The fun begins!” Yandra exclaims.

“Most humans only search for mates at nighttime, for whatever reason,” Orvius clarifies, “They have designated locations for seduction called ‘bars’ and ‘clubs’.”

He and Yandra shepherd us toward a grouping of silver panels against one far wall. Yandra reaches the panels first and presses a button between them with an upward pointing arrow marking it.

A *DING!* Sounds and Lochlynn and I both startle slightly, glancing around for its source.

One pair of silver panels open, revealing themselves to be doors, to a small cubical space. Three sides are transparent, providing the illusion that we've walked back out, into the throngs of bustling humans.

Yandra presses another button—this one marked with figures foreign to me—that is one of roughly fifty. With another ding, the panels slide closed.

With a unsettling lurch, our miniscule quarters suddenly lifts off the ground, carrying us up, up, up.

My head swims as I look out, over the endless expanse of city. I can see water in one direction—the Mississippi River from whence we arrived—and hundreds or thousands of other structures of human construction, most much shorter than the one we are currently scaling.

Yandra adds to our ongoing discussion, "Humans often consume substances at these 'bars' and 'clubs' which loosen their inhibitions, as well. We will use this to our advantage because—not only do they lower inhibitions—they also impair memory and the senses and decision making processes."

"Humans *purposely* lower their own inhibitions, impair their cognition, and dully their memory to search for mates?" I inquire, "Isn't that... counterproductive? How do they find mates with whom they have common interests, similar ethical leanings, compatible intelligence levels?"

"Oh, most don't." Orvious comments with a shrug, as our vessel continues to lift us toward the clouds, "That's not high on most of their lists of priorities, if truth is told. Most male humans simply strive to find the most attractive human who will settle to accept them, while most human females attempt to pair up with the human with the most financial resources and stability and luxury of lifestyle."

"How shallow..." Lochlynn comments with an expression of

distain, "Life must be so dull for these humans, once they find a mate."

The humans below are as tiny as plankton, indistinguishable from our height.

"Most find many, *many* mates and only stay with each for a few hours or perhaps days at a time." Yandra informs us, "They seek only to satisfy the flesh, not the soul—which will work in your favor. Most human males will not ask or expect more from you than that which you are already seeking from them."

'That which I'm already seeking from them...' I fight to stifle a literal, physical cringe and grimace.

"Why is this so difficult for me?!" I wonder, ashamed and guilty. My mother made this same sacrifice, two decades ago. And, two decades prior to that, her mother did so before her. And, *her* mother before her. *"So, why do I resent my duty so? Why am I so loathed to do what must be done?!"*

It's not as it I've ever been particularly picky in terms of sexual partners, either. Since the onset of puberty, I have been enamored with my own body; and I have always enjoyed sharing that passion. I've always felt an overwhelming fascination in the bodies of others, as well—mermaid, selkie, and sylph bodies alike—and, as princess, I've very rarely been denied exploration of my such curiosities. But, in many years of experimentation and discovery, I've realized one truth about my own sexual taste: I am not attracted to or satisfied by males of any species.

And, to further my displeasure in my mission, I find all humans particularly unattractive. They're so dull—no colorful, shimmering scales, no majestic fur pelt and magic, no ornate shells and pearls... What *do* they have to offer? Awkward, clumsy legs and bland, lack-luster skin...? Disappointing.

After an ascent that lasts nearly as long as swimming up the central channel of Lumeria Palace, our transparent ferry slows and finally comes to a stop. With another *DING,* the gleaming metal panels slide open once more to reveal an opulent entrance hall.

Orvius withdraws the black-and-gold rectangle from his human clothing and inserts it into a slot next to a large, black ingress, which swings open to reveal a lavish domicile within.

"Your penthouse suite, Princess Aegaea D'Lumeria," Yandra steps within and beacons us to follow with a sweeping gesture of her arm, "The finest in all the city."

"Calliope's tit!" I breathe the vulgar, common phrase, earning a shocked and slightly amused grin and series of rapid blinks from Yandra.

Orvius clears his throat, uncomfortably, and says in a stiff tone, "Very well. We will leave you to get settled in, Your Highness. The master suite is to your left—your sleeping quarters, my Princess—and accommodations for you, Commander Orca-Chaser, are beyond the door to our right. Should you require assistance of any sort," he gestures to a line of buttons on the wall by the door we've just entered from, "You can contact Yandra and I by pressing this button and speaking in your normal voice," his finger hovers over top button, "We are on the floor just below this one. And, just above us, on the roof, there is a swimming pool. A miniscule pool of water that the humans have treated with awful chemicals; however, should you find yourself overwhelmed and longing to feel your body submerged, it will do the trick."

"Thank you," I say in my sincerest tone.

Yandra and Orvius withdraw from our lodgings, leaving Lochlynn and I to ourselves.

Still awkward on my newfound legs, I place one in front of the other, forcing them to carry me to what seems to pass for a bed to humans. I allow my body to plop down on the springy surface, testing its buoyancy.

"My body feels so heavy," I mumble, wiggling the little nubs at the end of my legs, peeping out from the strange, bindings Yandra placed upon them after Lochlynn transformed my fin. I'd been told they're called 'shoes'. "The legs tire easily… especially where they bend."

Lochlynn nods and hums, "Mm-hmm," sympathetically, as she pokes around our quarters, inquisitively.

I slide the *'shoes'* off and lift the bottom of my leg—the part with the little wriggly nubs—and I twist myself around so that I can place it on top of the other leg and rub the soreness away.

"How do humans live this way?" I wonder, aloud.

"I suppose they get used to it," Lochlynn mutters, still peeking in all the drawers and cabinets.

"Could you stop that," I say, grinning, "And get over here and show me some attention, *please*? I could use a massage…"

Lochlynn glances over her shoulder at me, knowing as well as I that I am jesting, and grins as she says, "Yes, Your Highness, as you wish." She produces an exaggerated, mocking rendition of the honorary salute reserved for addressing the royal family—my family—during ceremonious occasions.

She crosses the room on more-practiced legs—the same legs she walks around Lumeria on, when in her most human-like state—and falls to her knees before me. She takes my appendage in her hand and begins rubbing the arching center.

Her thumbs move in firm circles along the bottom, creating a sensation unlike any my fin has ever given me... Like I might laugh... or pee... or *cum...*

My eyes roll back in my head and I close them, breathing deeply.

My slit—now between my legs, as opposed to the front of my fin—grows warm and wet. I can feel it leaking onto the garment that encases my legs, that moister growing cool as the air hits it.

Without warning, Lochlynn leans forward and places her lips around one of the little nups, sucking it, rubbing the underside with the top of her tongue.

I moan loudly, throwing my head back.

Lochlynn chuckles and moves to the next toe, taking her time there, as well. As she works her way across, sucking and licking each one, she continues to rub the arch with her thumbs.

Once she has thoroughly appreciated that one, she moves to the other leg and begins sucking on those and rubbing.

I moan and my clit throbs, begging for some of the attention. *Such a jealous little thing...*

My fingers rub between my legs, but I'm impeded by the thick fabric. I buck upward, frustrated, and grab at the garments, attempting to shed them.

"Sheesh," Lochlynn teases me, "Impatient, much?" She releases my leg and helps me out of my clothing.

As soon as I am free of my inconvenient attire, she grabs my legs just above the bendy parts and forces them apart as far as they will spread.

She begins right next to her hand where she holds my legs and begins kissing and nibbling across the soft, smooth flesh, making her way toward the middle...

I can feel my own fluids dripping along the crack between my legs, toward the bedding.

When she nears my most sensitive zone, she switches legs, earning a frustrated growl from deep within my chest.

She seems to move up my other leg even more slowly than the first one and another stream of me streams down the ravine...

I am whimpering, nearly breaking down to *beg*, by the time she finally reaches the slick, throbbing mound between my legs.

It is not covered in fur, as hers is in this state, but bares just a light dusting of tightly-coiled hairs, a fingertip's-width above my clit. As such, when I glance down to sneak a peak at her artful tongue-dance, the folds of flesh appear pink and glistening. My pearl stands at attention, hard and shiny, peaking out at her as she flicks just the very tip of her tongue against it, rapidly and unrelenting.

Her fingertip traces the rim of my cavern, teasingly, before dipping inside. Once inside, she realizes how slick and *ready* I already am, and another finger joins the first.

Lochlynn scissors her fingers open and closed inside me, stretching and massaging my inner walls, while her tongue laps greedily at the juices that flow from within, as though she fingers an overripe fruit. The thumb of her other hand presses against my clit and massages there, too.

My hands caress my ample breasts, twisting my erect nipples.

I watch her pelvic frolic for as long as I can stand to; but, eventually, I am overcome by ecstasy and my eyes roll back in my head.

I throw myself back on the bed, gasping and writing as wave after wave crashes over me.

My legs involuntarily close around Lochlynn's head, wrapping around her neck and draping down her back, holding her mouth and tongue to me as I rock back and forth, humping her face as each spasm sends stars of pleasure across my vision.

Knock, knock, knock!

Both Lochlynn and I jump and scramble to make ourselves decent.

"Y-yes?" Lochlynn inquires, "Who's there?"

"It's us, Your Majesty," Orvius's familiar voice answers, taunt with discomfort, "We heard... *noises...* I was concerned for your safety. It sounded as though someone were in distress..."

I snort into my hands at Lochlynn's mortified expression.

"Ur—No, no," Lochlynn stammers, "All's fine! All's good!"

"We need to soon head to supper," Yandra's amused voice tells us, "We have reservations and shouldn't be late, lest they give away our table."

Such seems unfathomable to me—I've *never* been treated in such an inconsiderate, inhospitable manner!—but, I take her for her word and begin fighting my way back into the human garments. After all, I'm not royalty here, on the surface. To any whose eyes land on me here, I am but a commoner... one of millions...

Lochlynn does the same and, once we are both decent, Lochlynn opens the door, glancing out, into the hallway to be sure no threats loom. When she sees only Yandra and Orvius, she holds the door open for me to pass. She follows right on my heels and pulls the door firmly shut behind her, testing the knob to be sure it has locked after. It has.

We follow Yandra and Orvius into the elevator, down the side of the building—gazing out across the city of New Orleans as the setting sun casts a golden glow across it—though the lobby, and out, onto the street filled with hurrying humans.

Music wafts through the air. It's not like anything I've ever heard in Atlantis. The notes seem to lean into one another, drunkenly. The rhythm drips with arousal and sensuality and I find myself walking more closely to Lochlynn than I would have dared to allow myself, back home.

But, with the freedom of anonymity, I allow myself the rare pleasure and my arm rubs against hers as we traipse along, following our guides.

Yandra and Orvius lead us a ways along the same street as our accommodations and through a doorway, into a multi-leveled structure filled with tables and chairs and too many human bodies to occupy them. Orvius speaks to a man at the door and he leads us to a table, though many humans seem to be waiting long before us.

This must be what Yandra meant by our *'reservation'* and our table possibly being given away upon our tardiness.

We are seated at a table covered in a spotless white cloth and our meals are promptly served. My dish comprises of a variety of small, aquatic crustaceans and is not as dissimilar from Atlantian cuisine as I would have assumed. The humans do seem to enjoy adding other flavors, though—

especially flavors that seem to set my mouth afire.

When we emerge from the crowded establishment, the sun has set. However, small orbs of light suspended above the streets and brightly-colored figures glowing above the doorways of various shops light the night to near daytime visibility.

The carnal tunes continue to coil through the air like a current, leading us, beaconing us, turning us at an intersection and guiding us down one strip more congested than any other we've passed.

Sweet, enticing smells waft from open doorways.

As we pass one establishment—steady, hypnotic thumps and bumps of bass music luring me closer—a woman with one of the grandest chests I've ever seen grabs me by the wrist and pulls me toward her.

Shocked, I freeze and do nothing to stop her as she throws her arms around me and squeezes her breasts to mine, the four thick mounds squishing together and shoving each other upward with her rhythmic thrusts.

I realize, a moment later, that she is dancing with me! A single hoot of laughter escapes my lips stretched tight over my teeth as I smile with pleasure. I move my body with hers, mimicking her gyrations, rubbing the skin of my cleavage—exposed by the deep V of my human garments—against hers.

The sensation sends a burst of warmth between my legs.

The human woman—whose garments expose even more skin than my own—reaches behind herself, where another woman stands with a tray of thin, glass tubes filled with a bright, green liquid, and plucks a vial and places it into her cleavage. Pulling her shoulders back and sticking her breasts in my face, she shouts over the music booming from within, "TAKE IT! ON THE HOUSE, SWEETHEART!"

I'm taken aback, confused, unsure of what she means. But, when I glance around for some indication of what she's expecting of me as she now stares at me, waiting, I see Yandra being treated similarly by another human woman. As I watch, she leans her face into that woman's cleavage, takes the vial in her teeth, and tosses back her head so that the liquid inside flows down her throat. She leans her head back down, swallowing, and the human woman takes the vial from her with her mouth, strikingly white teeth clamping on the end, just a finger's breath from Yandra's lips.

Yummmm…

I copy her actions, leaning my face into the woman's ample bosom, allowing my lips to brush against the smooth, warm skin, and I take the glass tube between my teeth.

I throw it back and the green liquid burns all the way down my throat.

I cough and gasp as the human takes the empty tube from me and moves on to her next partner.

I laugh as I turn back to Lochlynn, Yandra, and Orvius, "I think I'm going to like it here," I say, grinning like a dolphin with a pufferfish.

Chapter Four:
On The Prowl

Lochlynn

Yandra and Orvius keep a list of local establishments most suitable for finding potential mates for the mermaids who choose to come to shore to procreate—establishments which foster anonymous, one-time-only meetings between humans as a business model. Humans have various names for these establishments: bars, clubs, pubs, lounges.

For the future queen of our people, for obvious reason, that list was refined to only the safest, most secure, *most infiltrated* of those. Only those institutions owned and/or operated by non-humans; only those with measures in place to assure her safety and anonymity.

This narrowed their list exponentially.

A handful of locations were approved, however, including The Night Knight Cabaret and Burlesque Mascarade.

While the location might be owned by humans, the mastermind and manager, Etoile Theriot, is a witch born to a bayou coven very acquainted with our kind—as well as other nonhumans found on the surface and common to New Orleans—and quite sympathetic to various needs for human flesh...

It is in the dimly-lit masked audience of The Night Knight that we find ourselves, after a few failed stops at bars and clubs that Aegaea deemed '*apalling*' for reasons she refuses to disclose, sitting around a table sheathed in red silk and lit with only a single candle flame.

All around us, there are *dozens*—perhaps a hundred or more!—human men, primed and ready for the picking as they sit back and observe the night's entertainment.

Aegaea seems to pay them no mind, though.

Part of me is relieved. I had been so scared and disgusted by the thought of having to watch her with another... possibly multiple others.

But, the longer she takes to select one, the longer this nightmare drags on... and on, and on...

Yet, she only seems to have eyes for the human women on stage, singing their lungs out and performing coordinated, sexually-charged dances.

This is worse. So, so much worse.

At least, if she were doing her duty and searching out a human *male*, I could tell myself that she acts purely of obligation. But, as I sit back and observe her—gaze locked on one particular woman with hair nearly white and lips painted bright red—I cannot lie to myself; I can see the lust in her eyes.

She's not acting out of obligation; she's just horny.

And, what would some human *woman* have that *I* do not?

I can wrap my head around her need to provide an heir. I can even tolerate her various dalliances and affairs in Atlantis. Besides, none of her flings have ever lasted more than a few weeks. Others have come and gone, for both of us, but we never have.

For a princess who has never been denied a desire in her lifetime, she's actually incredibly selfless and giving—too much so, at times, but how can I begrudge her one of my favorite of her qualities?

We've enjoyed exploring one another's bodies since curiosity first struck as adolescents, but she and I have never officially placed any sort of label on our relationship, aside from lifetime friends. Aegaea has never expressed any sort of desire to have a monogamous relationship and, while our queens almost always declare a consort at some point in their life, marriage is not required for the princess to take the crown, or ever in her reign as queen.

I've never *expected* that I might receive that honor, though part of me can't help but dream.

My mother, on the other hand, is certain of my future and has her heart set on my someday becoming Queen Consort. She doesn't know Aegaea the way I do, though... Aegaea has never been one for sentimentality. She's more of a carnal being than a spiritual one...

And, in Atlantis, marriage is considered the *most* spiritual act. Love and sex are typically freely given; and, when not easily found, there are safe, regulated services available.

Most mermaids and sylphs aggressively spurn the idea of marriage and monogamous relationships and live polyamorously, having a small number of close partners who each fulfill a different set of needs. There are some who prefer to focus on other pursuits entirely, as well, and live celibately with a number of close platonic friends and family.

Somehow, Aegaea seems to fit into both these categories; I've never seen her as the marrying type. I can't even picture it.

We selkies are considered odd among the other peoples of the oceans for our beliefs regarding marriage and family. Family—and more specifically, the bonds of love that form marriage and families—are considered sacred to my people above all else.

The dancers leave the stage and I feel ill as the moon-haired goddess—gaze locked with Aegaea's behind delicate, intricate masks—makes her way toward our table.

She loops a long, fuzzy adornment around Aegaea's neck and leans in to flirtatiously run her long, talon-like fingernails up and down her arms, singing to her intimately as if serenading her alone in bed, not in a crowded room full of on-lookers...

My insides squirm and I tense, fully on guard.

This establishment is supposed to be safe, but my gut does *not* like anything I'm seeing...

Chapter Five:
Love in the Cabaret

Aegaea

I cannot get the memory of that first night in the city out of my head in the weeks to come… *that dance*…

The woman with hair like spun moonlight had caught my attention from the moment she had stepped into the spotlight. Her voice—nearly as magical as my own as she raised it to remarkable notes—warbled with vibrato unlike anything I've ever heard before. Her crooning brought tears to my eyes and made me feel things… sorrow and joy and tremendous love…

But, it wasn't just her song which captivated me; the ways in which she moved her body left me long—aching-—to reach out and… touch…

I could tell, just by observing the humans in the audience around me, that touching was something either highly frowned upon or downright forbidden, however. Every man and woman keeps their hands respectfully to themselves; so, that is exactly what I do, as well, as she loops her fluffy thingy around my neck and beacons her to me with her voice.

I gaze into her silvery-blue eyes as she croons her alluring melodies. She leans into me, her breath sweet and crisp in my nostrils and on my tongue as I breathe. Her chest nearly rubs against mine, but she manages to somehow keep a hair's distance from my skin as she rolls her body with the rhythm of the notes bellowed from her longs.

Her throat bobs up and down, visibly, as she raises her voice and lowers it to impressive octaves.

She has no qualms of touching my skin, so I figure the social rule must not go both ways in these situations and establishments. She runs her palms up and down my bare arms and along the edge of my jawline.

Too soon, she moves on to another member of the crowd at another table.

I resist the urge to beg her to come back. The number ends as I jealously watch her with another patron.

As the performers—my moonlight-maiden included—retreat behind the curtains of the stage as the music trails off and goes quiet for an intermission, Yandra grabs my attention, "Do any of the men in the audience capture your fancy?" She wiggles her eyebrows and glances around the room, "There are some excellent candidates here... genetically superior... Look at the muscles on *him*!"

I glance in the direction she nods and do, indeed, notice a human man dressed in a tight black-and-white garment, with thick hair and a dark stubble on his jaw. He looks just like every other man I've seen since arriving top-side.

I grunt and glance back toward the curtains where *she* disappeared...

"The men here seem to have eyes only for the performers, though," Lochlynn remarks, "Perhaps we should search out another establishment like the last, where the men were asking her to dance and trying to buy her drinks? At least they were attempting to gain her attention..."

"I thought she said *that* was—what word did you use, Your Majesty?—discomforting?" Orvius inquires, "We suggested The Night Knight so that *she* could select her choice. Once she makes a selection, we will have our *in* with management pull him aside and make the connection."

Lochlynn glances pointedly in my direction, then grunts, "She doesn't seem interested in *any* of the *men* here..."

I sigh. She's right. I'm not. They all look the same; they all *act* the same. The all want the same thing...

I've been here for more than two weeks. Eighteen nights of visiting every single establishment on Yandra and Orvius's list of suitable institutions—some twice—and, still, not one human male has stood out from the crowd.

I'd tried to bite the bullet a few times, since hope dwindles to find that special 'one' amongst them. I'm coming to realize that *that* was a damned myth. All little mermaid girls dream of coming to the surface, finding one man who stands out, one man so beautiful you want to see his face on your daughter, forever...

But, do I care what my baby looks like?

Not one damned bit.

I just want to go home... to go home, with Lochlynn, and begin our life, our family, our reign...

I've brought back to this room atop this overly-luxurious hotel two very optimistic, very *eager* men.

The first had hair nearly the same shade as Lochlynn's and I tried to focus on this attribute. I tried to close my eyes and *pretend...*

But, as he aggressively kissed my neck and collarbones, his bristly facial hair rubbing me raw, I found myself unable to just grit my teeth and get through the task.

Everything about the man turned my stomach—his smell, the firmness of his body and muscles, the scratchy texture of his palms and fingers as he rubbed the inside of my left upper leg, believing himself to be giving me something resembling pleasure.

I'd tried to salvage the situation by taking charge, only to have him tell me in an offended tone, *"I'm no pussy-boy sub, Baby. I'm a dom! I dominate. Just lay back and let me send you to another world of pleasure, Sweetie..."*

"Nope," I sat up, stood up, crossed the room, and opened the door for him, "Get out."

"What?" He gasped, offended, gawking at me, naked, sitting on the end of the bed, "You *can't* be serious?"

"*Dead* serious," I confirmed, "Just go."

"You're just going to send me away with *Blue Balls*!? You propositioned *me*, you bitch!" He stormed toward me, only to have Lochlynn—who he was unable see from his angle—lay him out on the ground by taking one step into the room, throwing her fist out, and allowing him to charge his nose right into it.

Orvius and Yandra had disposed of him while Lochlynn had *tended my emotional wounds*…

If you catch my drift…

It had taken me three nights to work up my courage to pick another human male to take back to the hotel room, and then only with the understanding that Lochlynn is to remain in-room for the duration to stand guard and protect me from whatever danger the next human male presented.

This second attempt had been chosen at little more than random, if truth be told; I couldn't name one feature he possessed ten minutes after throwing him out for his entitlement and lack of respect.

He insisted that Lochlynn join our activities, despite my repeated refusals, *her* repeated refusals, and my even explicitly outing her as my security detail.

He'd scoffed and retorted that a female security detail could not be effective. He'd called us liars and '*skanks*', '*prostitutes*' and '*scammers*', whatever those words mean…

His stay had been even shorter than the first. Lochlynn had enjoyed showing him just how effectual she can be as head of my security.

We traipse down the street I have been told is named 'Bourbon', toward one of the bars Yandra and Orvius has picked for us. This is our time visiting this particular location, and I'm not that excited as I wasn't impressed the first time with the sort of clientele drawn to it.

My eye is caught by the glimmer of moonlight hair as *she* ducks into a club across the street.

"Orvius!" I call, already turning to head across the busy street, "Yandra! We *need* to go in this one! C'mon!"

I dart across the road, despite their protests, Lochlynn running on my heels, and our guides are racing to catch up behind her, as they'd gotten a few paces ahead of us. They call out my name but I ignore all three of them, doing my damnedest to catch up with her.

The club in question has several colorful tapestries displayed in the windows, glowing rainbows of brilliant, fluid-like light hang above the doorway.

Orvius and Yandra manage to catch up to us just as Lochlynn reaches me, standing at the rear of an impressive line to get inside.

"Princess!" Yandra hisses, discreetly, "That was *very* dangerous!"

"This is not on the pre-approved list of safe venues!" Orvius whispers, panicking, "Hunting here could open us up to any number of untold dangers!"

"Calm down," I roll my eyes, "I just want to go in for a minute. We didn't have any luck at this place you're taking me to last week; what makes you think we will, this time? I like the look of the patrons here…"

It's true, even aside from the woman with the pale hair. These men are dressed in brighter colors. Some even have hair in colors more typical of mermaids or sylphs than humans. Some wear makeup to enhance their better features. The equipment worn on their feet is much more aesthetically pleasing…

"I can see what you mean," Lochlynn mumbles, glancing around, puzzled, "What makes these humans so… *colorful*… and, why do the colorful humans only seem to congregate at the colorful bars?"

"I'm not sure," Yandra remarks, shrugging, "We've only been told that they seem to have been much less successful in past hunts."

"Well," I grin, feeling optimistic for the first time in weeks, "*I'm* not *most* huntresses, now am I?"

I spin around as we reach the man permitting entry into the bar. Even he is wearing a shirt that is striped pastel pink, sky blue, and glittery in the middle. There are no sleeves on the upper garment, exposing thick arms rippling in muscles.

I wonder if I might find someone a bit more... *cuddly...* inside—although, he is one of the most attractive specimens I've seen yet.

Orvius presents the man in the striped shirt with four small, rectangular pieces of plastic, as well as flashes him something within a black casing and explains to him that I am the daughter of a foreign official and he, Yandra, and Lochlynn are my security. We are permitted entry, as well as gifted paper jewelry for our wrists which the man informs us will allow for access to the VIP section. He expresses gratitude that we have chosen his establishment to visit this evening.

I, too, am glad I happened to catch that glimpse of...

Her.

She's standing at the bar with three other women. All of them are tall and dressed in tiny garments, perched on thin spikes protruding from their heels. Each has a small parcel on a chain or string tossed delicately over one shoulder, or across their torso. All four are breathtakingly endowed and their tiny garments expose deep, plunging cleavage, while also nearly revealing the undersides of their round bottoms. Their hair and faces are impeccably done and each seems to possess all the confidence they are due.

Uncharacteristically, I'm brought up short by a bout of nerves. I pause halfway across the club, take a deep breath, run my hands along the contours of my own skimpy garments, and smooth my hair; then, and only then, do I find the courage to approach her.

"Hello," I say, my voice shaking almost imperceptibly. I hold out my hand as I've observed other humans doing in bars and clubs in these situations, "I'm Aegaea. I think I saw you perform a couple of weeks ago, at The Night Knight?"

"Oh, yes! I remember you, Hunny!" She beams at me, revealing sparkling, unearthly white teeth behind lips painted purple, "What a coincidence, running into you again! Hi! I'm Ann."

Ann. What a simple, elegant, perfect *name for such a complicated, sophisticated woman*...

"Y-yeah! I-I, urm, I wanted to tell you how much I enjoyed your performance." I stammer, "I'm sorry my security made me leave right after... Your voice... it's... *wow...*"

"Oh, gosh!" Ann gushes, embarrassed and flattered. She glances around at her friends and they all fall away, taking her meaning, "Thank you! That's too sweet! You're just too sweet! So, do you live in the city? Are you from here? I've never seen you in here, before, or at The Night Knight before the other night, and I'm either here or there, like, *every night...*" She laughs and the sound is like the morning call of seagulls, full of hope and life and peace...

"No, no," I lament, "I'm only here for a few weeks. I will have to leave soon..."

Her face falls, "What a shame," she mourns, "I'm always happy to make new friends, but I'm always sad when they have to leave New Orleans after Mardi Gras."

"Mardi Gras?"

"Yeah," Ann pauses, "Sorry, I just assumed, since it's that time of year and you said a few weeks... Are you here on business, then?"

"Oh, uh, yeah," I stammer, feeling more awkward that I ever have in my life, "Something like that..."

"Would you like a drink?" she asks, but doesn't wait for an answer, before assuming my answer and asking her follow-up question, "What are you having? Bartender!"

"Oh, uh, what do you suggest?"

She strings together words that make no sense together to me, but the bartender seems to know exactly what sort of drink to mix as he starts selecting bottles immediately.

She turns back to me and immediately says, "So? You enjoyed the show?" She's fishing for more compliments, but I'm more than willing and able to dole them out.

"Absolutely," I say, truthfully, "You were breath-taking. Spectacular. I'm a singer, too," I dare to venture to tell her, "So, I know more than most, even, how technically perfect you were..."

She laughs, surprised, "Well, that really *does* stroke my ego! Most of the time I just get tourists who tell me who attractive I am..."

"Well," I shrug, "I figured as much. I can plainly see you wouldn't lack for flattery and attention. Any fool can tell you how beautiful your face and body are, or how your hair shines like moonlight on the ocean... Not many could tell you, from my experience, how spell-binding, how *enchanting* your voice is."

"R-really?" her face flushes and she nearly swoons, adulated, "You thought *that* much of *one song*?"

"I thought that much of one note," I say, leaning in to reach across the bar from her and take the drink offered by the bartender, "You are immensely blessed."

"Thanks," she glances away, her face darkening even more, and sips her own drink. She brushes a strand of her long, shimmering hair from her face.

"I'd lo—"

I'm not sure to what end, but I'm about to invite her back to my accommodations; but, alas, Lochlynn finally catches up and interrupts us, "Aegaea! You need to stop trying to ditch us… *Oh*…" Her gaze lands on Ann and I can see the recognition as it splashes across her face.

"Lochlynn, this is Ann," I make the introduction, "If you remember her from The Night Knight? Ann, this is my Head of Security, Lochlynn."

"Head of Security," Ann mumbles, looking Lochlynn up and down, thrown, "Are you, like, a celebrity, or something? Should I know you?"

"Or something," I chuckle, "I supposed to be here looking for… a *date*." I use the word that humans seem to use in place of blatantly vocalizing a desire for sex.

"Oh, really?" She seems intrigued, "A date to what, may I ask?"

This throws me; I'm not sure what answer she's seeking or what's appropriate. Instead of responding, I wink at her and trail my gaze across the club, "I like it here," I state, "Everyone is so… *vibrant.*"

"Aye," Lochlynn frowns, perplexed, then whispers to me, "But none of the men seem all that interested, just as Yandra and Orvius predicted. The only one to spare either of us a second glance has been *Ann*, here…"

I can't help myself; I allow my gaze to dart back to Ann at Lochlynn's mention.

She's staring at us, absorbing our conversation and confused by it, "Umm," she blinks a few times, batting those remarkably thick lashes, "*Men*?

You're... wait... you're trying to pick up *men*? *Here*?!"

Lochlynn, befuddled, turns back to Ann, "Yes, what of it?"

"Well, you're not going to have much luck. This is a gay bar... I thought you must know that, based on how hard you were flirting with me, just now...?" She continues to frown and blink at me in confusion.

"A what?" Lochlynn asks.

"A *gay bar*," She repeats, thought the phrase to us means nothing more than a '*happy*' bar, "Everyone here is queer." Upon seeing our increasingly blank expressions, she continues to try to explain, "The women are looking to hook up with other women; and, the men are looking to hook up with other men... and, then you have the transmen and transwomen, like me..."

"A *what*-woman?"

I feel my head tilt to the side. Relationships between female selkies and mermaids, two mermaids, female sylphs and mermaids, and any combinations thereof—or selk males with sylph males, for that matter—are far from unheard-of, taboo, or even treated any differently in Atlantis. There is no need for 'gay' establishments, as relationships between two females or two males outnumber those between a male and a female of any given species.

"A *trans*woman..." She squints at me in what seems to be effort to discern whether I am mentally incompetent... "I was born genetically male... *down there*?"

"You," I struggle to comprehend, though I have a very intriguing image in my head in that moment, "So, you're a woman with the... *equipment* of a human male?"

"Uh," She changes her body language just slightly, tilting herself away from me, "*Yeah*...?"

"That's incredible!" I can't stop myself from exclaiming, "Wow! That's... that's like... *you're* like... *oh, wow,* you're like the best of both... you're perfect!"

She seems bewildered by my reaction, "What do you mean? I'm not some *fetish*..."

"No!" my stomach drops, disgusted that she could take my meaning as such, "No! That's *not* what I mean… I… well, this is *really* hard to explain… I hope I haven't offended you. I'd love to—I don't know—go somewhere we can talk? Somewhere quieter?"

The steady beating of the music inside this club is slightly different than the other clubs, but still extraordinarily loud.

"S-sure?" She relents, after several moments spent staring directly into my eyes, searching for any ill intent and, presumably, finding none, "I know a little coffee shop right up from here that is tucked in a corner and missed by most of the tourist. Would you want a frappe?"

I have no idea what a frappe is, but I immediately spout, "Yes! I'd *love* that!"

Chapter Six:
The Goddesses from Atlantis

Ann Birchwick

'Who the actual fuck is this chick?!' I wonder as I lead Aegaea, Lochlynn—Aegaea's Head of Goddamn Security—and two—yes, *two!*—additional security officers toward my favorite bistro.

The male security officer asks what I would like as the unnamed female one shepherds us toward an lonesome table in a corner.

Aegaea, Lochlynn, and I sit around the small table while the unnamed woman goes to stand at the exit to guard the café, and us.

The man brings our frappes, then proceeds to stand with his back against the wall next to our table, staring across the room at his counterpart by the door.

"So..." I glance between the two gorgeous women sitting across from me, willing myself to ignore the officers, "Where are y'all from? Your accents are so unusual... I'm not sure I've ever heard any quite like them..."

"Urm," Aegaea stammers and glances toward Lochlynn, squirming uncomfortably in the wrought-iron chair, "You're probably not familiar," she blows off my question, "A very small, typically-overlooked nation far, *far* across the ocean..."

"Which ocean?"

I watch as both women glance toward the closest security detail—the man—before ignoring my question entirely.

"Where did you learn to sing like that?" Aegaea redirects the question, batting her thick—though seemingly natural—lashes at me.

My heart leaps in my chest at the possibility that she finds me as breathtaking as I find her as I stare into her honey-gold eyes. Her complexion is as smooth as a living TikTok filter, her lips deep mahogany—a stain, maybe? Definitely not a lipstick or gloss... Her hair is just as impeccable but—as far as my *very* discerning eye can see—completely *au natural.*

'The body and volume are spectacular... I wonder what products she uses...'

I shake myself just a bit as I remember that she is waiting for a response from me. "Oh, um, I was in all the clubs and ensembles in school—drama, glee, choir, jazz... I had more music teachers than I could give credit to. You said you're a singer, too?" I notice Lochlynn shoot Aegaea a reproachful glance, and I am thrown for a moment, before finding my way back to the tracks of my train of thought, "Do you perform? Are you a recording artist? Can I look you up on Spotify?"

"Ur..." She blinks, a completely blank glaze washing over her face that tells me she hasn't understood some part of my questioning, though it all seems pretty straightforward to me, "I... no?"

"How have you never heard of Spotify? The music app? Kind of like iTunes? You know iTunes? Right? What, are you, like, time travelers? Aliens? Of the extra-terrestrial sort?"

Aegaea and Lochlynn both glance fearfully toward the other two security agents, then at each other.

They lean into one another and a whispered exchange takes place behind Lochlynn's hand and Aegaea's hair as it flops in front of her face. I am unable to make out several breathy phrases.

After the briefest of secret conversations, Lochlynn sighs, rolls her green eyes, sits back a bit in her chair, and hisses, "*Fine*! Go. But you'd better not be one second after sunrise returning to our accommodations. It'll be *my* skin and job *your mother* will come for if something happens to you..."

"I know, I know!" She gushes, grinning ear-to-ear, "Thank you!" She leans in and pecks her Head of Security on the lips—taken me by surprise and turning me on so much so that I worry my tucking panties might not be doing their job and I cross my legs underneath the table to maintain my feminine poise—then turns to me, eyes wild with excitement, "Let's go," she whispers to me.

"What? Where?" I ask, glancing around, at the two security guards, unable to stop myself.

"*Anywhere*!" She practically trills as she grabs my hand and yanks me from my seat, "Just run! Go, go, *GO*!"

She pulls me along as she rushes past the unnamed woman guard and out onto Bourbon Street.

Hand-in-hand, shoving past the throngs of tightly-packed tourist bodies, laughing and yelling like maniacal banshees, we flee her considerable security detail.

We turn the corner, onto Canal Street, still at a full run; though, when I glance over my shoulder, I can find no trace of any of the three of them following.

I spin on my heels and yank her down a small side alley and into a little dive bar I've not frequented since transitioning.

We are two of only five patrons; the other three consist of a couple in a booth and a middle-aged, bald man slumped over the bar, barely-conscious.

The tourists would think he's some exotic Cajun local glued to this spot every night; I remember him to be the owner and I know that, while he is—in fact—here every night, sprawled out on the bar, it's all an act. He's as sober as a judge and willing and able to handle any mischief that the tourists might think up.

I ignore him; he wouldn't recognize or remember me.

I steer Aegaea to one of the four unoccupied booths and we sit down.

"What was all *that* about?!" I demand, laughing from the exhilaration, "Are you going to tell me why we just ditched your security guards? Why you *kissed* your Head of Security?"

Aegaea laughs loudly; the sound is contagious and I laugh with her.

"Lochlynn is… well… she's *more* than my Head of Security? Or, rather, who she is to me is *why* she's my Head of Security? She's been my best friend since diapers, and more since adolescence."

"So, she's your partner? Your girlfriend?"

"I suppose those words do describe our relationship… One day, she shall be my Consort, the other mother to my child."

"You're pregnant?"

"No," she sighs a heavy sigh, "Not *yet*, anyway… It's quite complicated. That's why I'm here, to… *conceive.*"

"Oh, like at a sperm bank?"

"A… a what?" She blinks those intense lashes at me, completely cluelessly.

"A fertility clinic?"

Still, nothing. No spark of recognition in her honey eyes.

"Then… *how* do you plan to get pregnant, here in New Orleans? Why did you travel *here* to do it? Don't you have fertility doctors in your home country?"

"No," she shakes her head, frowning, "There are *medical* doctors, who impregnate females? Human females?"

"Wh-why do you say it... like that? But, yeah... it's a whole field of medicine. How third-world *is* your country, Aegaea?"

"Third world? No, no," She shakes her head, "We are quite advanced, in technology *and* medicine. As I understand it, we are a bit more advanced that hu—" she freezes, blinks, then backpedals, "Than *New Orleans...eans?*"

"What are you talking about?" I feel like I am speaking to a *literal* alien. Like, E. Freaking. T. "Where the *fuck* are you *from*?!" I demand, in a hushed but forceful whisper.

She pauses for a moment, weighing her options and seeming to arrive to a conclusion of 'why-the-hell-not?', because she shrugs, and blurts out, "Atlantis."

"What?"

"Atlantis. More specifically, Lumeria Palace. I'm the Crowned Princess, Aegaea D'Lumeria, soon to be Queen Aegaea D'Lumeria. I am a siren."

"What?"

"*Your Highness*!" We both jump a bit as the door of the bar crashes open behind me. When I spin around, I find the unnamed female guard rushing toward us, slightly out of breath and panting, face red and eyes wild. "Up! Now! We are going back to your room and we will be contacting your mother *first* thing! Fleeing your security could have proven *disastrous*!"

Aegaea stands up, hands on her hips, and addresses the woman, "You'll be doing no such thing. I will mention this incident and your blatant insubordination tomorrow morning. In less than a year, *I* will be your queen. I am no child and I will not be treated as such. Should I decided to venture off, unaccompanied, that is up to *my* discretion and no one else—especially not you, *Lieutenant* Yandra, when I already approved the deviation from plans with your commander. Now, for your information, I am sharing a meal with the human whom I very likely might chose to genetically contribute to my daughter's conception. If you don't mind, I'd prefer a bit of intimacy and privacy as I get to know her and make that determination."

Lieutenant Yandra sputters and gawps at Aegaea, confuddled and blibbering, "Bu—*how*...? She—you—both women?!"

I chuckle, although it's absurd to think of anyone not at least a familiar with the *concept* of a transgender person, whether they agree or what their beliefs are... but, if Aegaea is telling the truth—and, it's hard not to believe her when she's so unearthly beautiful and so vastly alien in mannerisms—perhaps she never *has* experienced a transperson...? "Don't worry," I lean back in my chair and cock a grin, spreading my legs from their previous crossed position, "I'm *capable*..."

The baffled Yandra retreats from the bar and Aegaea bursts into laughter. "That was *perfect*!" she gushes, "I couldn't have come up with a better response, myself!" She blushes, glancing away, her eyelashes fluttering charmingly, "Sorry to just...

throw you to the sharks, so to speak..." She giggles nervously, "And, sorry to just *spring* that whole 'genetic contribution' bit... That's why I'm here. That's the whole reason—I have to conceive a child. There are no male sirens, or mermaids; and, we cannot mate with selkies—like Orvius and Lochlynn—nor Sylphs, like Yandra. So, we are forced to venture to the surface and seduce human... *males*... or, at least, until today, we've *thought* we were limited to males. What a revelation! HA!" she exclaims, overjoyed, "I've found human men to be quite repulsive, honestly. Males, in general—whether they be selk, sylph, or human—have never sparked much interests from me..."

"You're a lesbian," I state, shrugging.

She frowns, unfamiliar with any of our labels. "We mermaids and sirens do not believe in limiting ourselves to *one* mate for live—like selks and some humans seem to be inclined. As queen, I will be expected to choose a consort to help me raise the next air and carry out various duties of my position. I've always planned to crown Lochlynn. She's been my *special* partner—one of many, but also comparable to none—and the only person under the sea that I cannot fathom life without. But..." She trails off, her eyes darting between mine, glittering in the bar-light.

"But...?"

"But," She swallows, then whispers, "The moment I set eyes on you... the moment I heard your voice..." she shakes her head, ever so slightly, "I knew *you* were special, too. I knew *you* aren't like *anyone* I've ever met..."

"You—what?—want me to father your child and then let you disappear, forever, back to the sea? Never get to see the baby grow up?"

Aegaea blinks at me, her shoulders falling just a bit as she predicts my answer. She leans across the table and takes my hands as they rest on the table, clenched into fists.

"You want to use me for my body," I state, re-framing her request so that she might see it from my point-of-view, "and, not just *any* part of my body, but the *one* part I *despise.* The one part I've been saving every penny for ten years to have some doctor chop off?" My throat grows tight and my false nails bite into my palm, "No, thank you."

I yank my hands from hers and stand up, shoving my chair back.

With one last glance at the *goddess* I'm too scared to love, I practically run out of the bar.

Chapter Seven:
A Fish Out of Water

Aegaea

I drag myself back to the accommodations shared by Lochlynn and I, brokenhearted and angry.

I tap the door and Lochlynn swings it open, permitting me entry. "So?" She inquires, hesitant dread in her tightened eyes contradicting the flippant nature of her voice, "How'd it go?"

"She did not go for it," I shrug, attempting to downplay my vast disappointment and shame, "I guess I scared her off."

"Oh," She blinks, then feigns sympathy to hide her relief, "I'm sorry, Gea..."

"Yeah, well," I plop down on the foot of the bed and begin removing my shoes, "Her loss. I did, however, learn quite a bit from her. There are human *women* who possess the required parts and ability to impregnate. The humans call these women '*trans*'women. I believe I should narrow my search to these sorts of humans, since the males are just... *ugh*." I shudder.

"That's..." she pauses, searching my eyes while also trying to wrap her mind around it, "actually a huge step forward. That's *great*. I'm glad you've found a way to accomplish your royal sanction without having to put yourself through something you find repulsive."

"Thank you," I breathe a sigh of relief that she can see this situation from my point of view.

I lean into her, wrapping my fingers around the back of her neck, locking in the mattlocks there and pulling her face to mine. I press my lips to hers, parting them with my tongue and running it along the upper side of hers.

She moans and sinks into my kiss, relaxing her jaw and rubbing my shoulders as she kisses me back, massaging away the tension of rejection.

She uses her hands on my shoulders to guide me backward, further onto the bed, and then press me into the cloud-like pillows.

She looms over me, a knee at each of my hips and her hands by each of my ears, as she continues to kiss my lips, my jaw, my neck...

She takes her time on my breasts. She's always found them comforting yet entertaining—her words, long ago—and she is in no hurry, now. She nibbles each rigid peak softly, at first, taking turns and compensating with her fingers with the nipple not between her gentle teeth, their edges tantalizingly sharp...

"Oww—mmm," I gasp, then moan, as she bites just hard enough to surprise me and leave the sensitive flesh smarting.

She releases her dominion over my bosom to focus upon the garments that conceal my lower half from her easy access—*definitely* the worst part of life top-side, in my earnest opinion—yanking them down my waist and bottom, then tugging them down my legs and, finally, free of my body entirely. She tosses them across the room before grabbing me by the shins and forcing my legs apart.

She does not linger on ceremony tonight and, instead, dives tongue-first into my folds.

She can find my pearl with more ease than her own, even in this strange, human body, and she immediately begins flicking it aggressively. With her left hand, she parts my abundant flesh to give easier access to her tongue; with the index and middle fingers of her right, she plunges into me deepest core.

I gasp and moan, clenching my eyes shut as she brings me near climax with practiced ease and remarkable speed. As my back arches and my breath gathers within my chest, unwittingly and unwillingly, the piercing silver-blue eyes, moonlight tresses, vivid lips and strikingly-white smile of Ann slip into my mind's eye...

Chapter Eight: Kind

Ann

"Where'd you run off to?" Ysabella asks when I return to the bar.

"Yeah," intones Amber, "We just *knew* you were about to end up on The First 48, running off with strangers like that..."

"Ain't you ever heard of human trafficking, Girl?!" Keyrstan throws back a shot and hisses from the sting.

"They were pretty cool, actually," I say, glancing back at the entrance of the club, hoping to see Aegaea running after me to try to change my mind... I'm not even sure why I turned her down... I've always wanted to be a parent—just, on *my* terms and definition—but not only in biology. I would want to be part of any potential baby's life; and, how could that be remotely possible, if little Jr. is a freakin' mermaid?! *Or, siren, or whatever-the-fuck. Kinda wish I'd stuck around long enough to get some clarification there...* "Kinda wish I'd gotten her number..."

"You ran off, stayed gone for damn-near an hour, and didn' get no number? Girl, what *were* you doin' all that time?!" Kyrstan jibes, insinuating the kind of nasty shit she'd be liable to actually do...

"Talking," I remark, shrugging and feeling a hard lump in my throat when my siren-queen-in-shining-armor doesn't appear magically in the bar, begging me to reconsider.

Truth be told, I'd reconsidered the moment I turned the corner back onto Bourbon Street. It was stubbornness and pride that continued to place one foot in front of the order and carry me back to the queer bar where I'd first met Aegaea and abandoned my girl-friends.

"Wanna go out for a smoke?" Ysabella suggests.

When a general consensus is obvious in the nod of every other head, we head out onto the back patio to share a blunt.

"Did you know her, or somethin'?" snoops Amber.

"No," I answer her, taking a deep draw of the thin, brown, hand-rolled cannabis cigar, "She saw me perform a few nights ago at The Night Knight and when she happened to see us entering tonight, she decided on a whim to come meet me and let me know how much she enjoyed my performance."

"Ooooh," Ysabella drones, "Why *didn't* you get her number?! Why didn't you take her home?!"

"It's... complicated," I sigh, feeling a familiar darkness weighing on me, "*I'm* complicated. Let's just get completed faded, okay?"

Chapter Nine: Homesick

Lochlynn

I am thoroughly enjoying myself as I devour the juices dripping from my lover's gleaming, subtle, delicately pink flesh.

Aegaea raises her hips to meet my mouth and tongue, yearningly. She grabs hold of my locks and she pulls me into her, pressing my face into her.

As my tongue slips in and out of her warm, slippery hole, I open my eyes and glance up Aegaea's voluptuous body, expecting to meet her watching gaze, like so many times before...

Only to find her eyes clenched shut and her other fist jammed into her own mouth.

"You are thinking of her!" I whine, sitting back and wiping my mouth. Tears sting my eyes and my throat feels tight. Anger at my own display of emotion burns hot in my cheeks as I grind my teeth and blink the burning droplets away. "What does *she* have that I do *not*?! After all these years, how could a pretty new face steal your heart away so easily?!"

"What?" She sits up, frowning in genuine bewilderment, "What are you talking about, Lochlynn?"

"You know precisely what—and *who*—I'm talking about!" I snap, wiping more tears away with my forearm, "That '*trans*'-human-woman! Ann! Or, whatever her name was! You've not opened your eyes once since I started; and, you *always* like to glance down and watch every now and then! You don't think I notice, but I *do*. *Tides!* I sound like a whiny, insecure selk-kit with her first love!"

"Am I not?" Aegaea surprises me with three senseless words.

I attempt to make meaning of them but cannot, "What?"

"Am I not your first love?"

"Yes," I growl, "Of course you were! Are! But, I *was* under the impression we were different in that you would also be my *last*!"

"Can I not still be? Do you suddenly not love me?" Her chin trembles at the thought and she reaches out for me.

I shirk her touch and growl, "Of course I do! I wasn't the one fantasizing about someone else! It is *you* who no longer feel the same for me!"

"Where do you come by *that* notion?" She sits back, frustrated, "Have I not *always* taken loves, back at Lumeria Palace? Are we not here, topside, to perform a duty which we've *always* known I have been charged with? An enterprise which requires the... *aid* of someone... *like* Ann?"

"A man!" I retort, though I'm can hear the ridiculousness in my words, "You were supposed to find a *man*!"

"Why does it matter? She can accomplish the mission; and, as an added bonus, she doesn't make me want to recoil from every touch... Would you truly rather I force myself to endure something unstomachable to me, needlessly, to spare your ego? Why are you so much more jealous of Ann than any other mermaid, sylph, or selk I've slept with?"

"Because none of *them* have any stake in our future together."

"What do you mean?"

"You two obviously share a... *connection*. It was obvious the moment you set eyes on her, even before you knew she could give you a child. If she becomes the other mother of your daughter, where does that leave me? You'll take *her* for your Queen Consort... my family struggles so, since Father's death. My mother is relying on not having to worry about where she will sleep or what she will eat or how she will survive, when she is too old to work her job in the palace's kitchen. My sister and brother are relying on me to provide for them, when that time comes, until they get on their own feet... I don't want them to end up in social housing."

"It is not so bad," She tries to assure me, but not in the way I'd have liked, "My grandmother and mother have made enormous improvements to our safety nets for those sorts of situations... but," She reaches across the bed and turns my face back toward her, "Trust me when I say I'd *never* let any of that happen..."

"We're not your charity case," I growl, leaning away so that she cannot reach my face and standing up. Tears roll down my face as I realize that, deep down, I actually had gotten *my* heart set on being her partner for life, too... My heart feels as though it is literally breaking in my chest, aching in a tight squeeze, "*I* will provide for them. I thought we were a partnership and *we* would take care of them, and be a big, happy family, but I know now I'm delusional. I should have known better. Mermaids don't even believe in family loyalty. You'll just give your hearts and bodies to anyone who smiles in your direction!"

I spin on my heels and stomp out of our room, throwing open the door to the emergency stairs and beginning the wild, dizzying downward spiral of several dozen flights of stairs.

Chapter Ten: Loose Lips

Aegaea

I hurriedly re-dress myself in the strange, snug-fitting human garments and rush out of our accommodations, calling her name, "Lochlynn! Lochlynn?!" I find no trace of her, though, and rush down the dizzying multitude of flights of stairs.

When I step out onto the street known as Canal Street, I look one way then the other, searching for her towering, yellow-haired head above those of the humans. I see no sign of her, to my dismay, and I fruitlessly—and to many concerned glances and reproachful glares from the human crowd—scream her name, at the top of my lungs, exercising the full prowess of my Siren's Song in the two syllables.

Still, even after I wait nearly a full minute, I receive no response.

I stomp my foot in frustration, and I stalk off, in the direction I sense will lead me to the closest large body of water: the large lake that kisses the sea at its eastern-most point, named Pontchartrain by the humans.

Nearly three hours later, I reach a large pier.

The sun will soon rise. The sky above the gleaming waters is tinged pink and lavender and gold.

The long wooden pathway spans across the lake, raised above the water on beams like dozens of legs. At the end, far across the water, above the lake, there is a large structure of human architecture. The pointed roof and boxy shell of the construction make it feel so otherworldly and aesthetically displeasing to my eye. It is a blight on the beauty that is a vast surface of water reflecting the sunrise above...

But, where the wooden walkway meets the surface ground, there is a small strip of sand and upon it sits a small pack of women.

The final rays of moonlight glint off white hair and I freeze as my heart lurches in my chest, setting off a sensation in my belly that reminds me of a disrupted school of tiny fish. Shocked by the improbability and serendipity, I almost don't believe my eyes as they land on her face or my ears as they hear her musical voice ringing out in laughter.

Ann.

What an odd sense of humor the gods and goddesses and Fates have, I ponder as I nearly sprint across the final stretch of broken road to reach the tiny beach and my newest obsession on tired, aching feet, *Here I walk for miles in hopes of finding Lochlynn, righting my wrongs with her, and continuing on my set course of planned actions... only to find the temptress herself—my beckoning light in the dark, murky depths—Ann.*

This must be a sign, I rationalize the actions I know I cannot control, *this is fate...*

Her cluster of feminine companionship are not the only

humans milling about; there are dozens of men—and a few women—with fishing poles and gear walking toward and out onto the wooden structure. Many automobiles—as I've learned the humans refer to their version of our pods—roll up and down the busy street adjacent. Yet, I could not miss her, even where she and her friends sit, in the deep shadow cast by the pier.

"Ann?" I call across the beach, yelling above the sound of the lake's waters splashing at the sand and boardwalk.

Chapter Eleven:
Sink Ships

Ann

I glance up, mid-laugh at Ysabella's latest one-liner, to see none other than my little mermaid! My stomach and heart both begin doing summersaults. My specially-designed concealing panties become uncomfortable as other parts of me acknowledge her presence just as dramatically.

Like a magnetic pull, I feel an irresistible need to leap to my feet and step forward to greet her, a smile stretching my cheeks just as involuntarily. "Hey, You!" I call, elated. I turn back to my girls—whom I've spent the entire long walk out to the pier from the club telling *almost* all about my newest crush—and I make their introductions, "Amber, Ysabella, Kyrstan, *this* is Aegaea! Aegaea, these are my friends, Amber, Ysabella, and

Kyrstan…" I ramble their names off, awkwardly, earning myself the unabashed, knowing grins of my little posse.

"Hello," Aegaea greets them, her face open and friendly, though I can discern hesitant nervousness in her eyes, "So nice to meet you all."

"Same to you," remarks Kyrstan.

"Nice to meet you, too!" chimes Amber.

"So," it's Ysabella—characteristically—to ask the question, "Where are you from, Aegaea? I love your name, by the way. It's so… *exotic… Aegaea…* Is that after the goddess Gaea?"

"And the Aegean Sea," Aegaea smiles, proudly, "Thank you for the compliment."

"Did you choose it yourself, like the rest of us?" Ysabella pries further, fishing for information, "Or, is it a traditional name, where you're from? Your accent is… *lovely.*"

"Thank you," Aegaea repeats, "My mother and grandmother named me at my birth. We are a… *sea-faring* nation and peoples; so, yes, in a way, my name is traditional. It is quite common to name our daughters in ways that pay homage to the seas or to the divine."

The girls share a glance.

I do my best to divert the conversation away from Aegaea, to alleviate some of the anxiety I am reading in her eyes, "Ysabella isn't from here, either," I tell her, "So, don't let her make you feel like any more of a foreigner than she is!"

"So, where *exactly are* you from?" Ysabella asks again, with emphasis.

"What's with the third degree?" I intercept, on Aegaea's behalf, "Y'all are gonna run her off! C'mon, Aegaea," I loop my arm in hers, delicately, and lead her away from the girls, across the sand, "Let's go somewhere we can chat *sans* interrogation by these hoes!" I laugh as I lead her down the sandbar, toward the pier.

Behind us, I can hear them laughing and whooping and whistling after us.

When the water level is low, there are several yards of sandbar underneath the pier, where lovers often sneak away to canoodle. When the water is as low as it is tonight, there's enough headroom for even one so tall as I to walk easily and upright beneath.

"So," I lean against one of the algae-covered support beams and cock an eyebrow at her, "What? Are you stalking me? How the *hell* did you find me, all the way out here?"

Aegaea laughs, her cheeks flaring dark red, "In truth, it wasn't *you* I was seeking. Though, the coincidence *is* a happy one. I was searching for Lochlynn. She stormed out of our accommodations and disappeared into the crowd of New Orleans. I thought she might follow the innate pull we all feel toward the sea, the pull *I* felt... the pull that led me here, to this beach and this pier... to *you*..."

"This isn't the sea," I tell her, my gaze trapped in her honey-hued eyes, "It's a lake. Lake Pontchartrain. It connects to the sea, but..."

"I know," she says, her eyes never relinquishing mine, "I think the pull I felt was to you…" Aegaea confirms what I've suspected, though her frown is as confused as I feel, "Though, *why*, I have no clue…"

"Do sirens believe in fate? Or, destiny? Or, like, soulmates?" I ask, feeling my own face burning from a blush. I feel ridiculous and silly even saying the words—like I'm thirteen and pimply and swooning over some teen popstar heartthrob.

"No," Aegaea tells me, "We often keep many lovers and do not expect monogamy from any of them, in return, either. This is the philosophy of most mermaids—including sirens—and sylphs. But, selkies *do.* In fact, I think that's the source of the current misunderstanding between Lochlynn and I. She not only expects to become my Queen Consort—my partner in ruling Atlantis and in raising my daughter and, in life, in general—but also my *only* lover and relationship. This is the way of *her* people and the dynamics of their families; but, you see, this is *entirely* out of character for *my* kind... And, entirely impossible, when I am expected to provide an heir to the throne..."

"And, that's why you're here, right?" I surmise, from our earlier conversation, "To find a human to conceive a child with? Why can't you get some lucky mer-man to impregnate you?"

"Because there *are* none." She states, "There hasn't been a male mermaid or siren born in hundreds of years."

"What about that guy on your security detail?" I ask, confused.

"He's a selk," she informs me, "And, unfortunately, our genetic makeups are too different and selkies and mermaids are unable to reproduce. Same with Sylph males. But, for whatever reason, humans have DNA close enough to ours for procreation. So, every generation, the next siren queen comes to the surface to find a human male to father the next princess. Which, is a challenge in itself, and acutely dangerous. Trips to the surface aren't that uncommon for *common* mermaids; in fact, there are agencies in place to aid and protect them while top-side. However, for obvious reasons, sending our *only* princess and future queen to a foreign land could prove disastrous, especially since there are enemies of our crown... So, it is imperative that I '*perform my duty*' and return home, in one piece, and the sooner the better. But, there's one tiny problem..."

She hesitates and I see a pain behind her eyes.

"What?" I ask, intrigued.

"I am..." she sighs a heavy sigh, "I am *repulsed* by all the human males I've met! They are impulse-driven, condescending *beasts*!"

I laugh, relating on so many levels, "Tell me about it!"

"Well," she draws a huge breath, preparing a story, but I interrupt her.

"That's okay," I wave my hand, "I didn't mean that literally; I only meant that I know *exactly* what you're getting at. I will take your word for it and not make you relive whatever atrocities they've subjected you to."

"Good," she grinds her teeth, but then meets my eyes and relaxes her jaw, "Then, I met you… you're by far the most stunning human I've ever laid eyes on. I thought I was being distracted from my mission by your beauty, but when I learned you are *literally* the living incarnation of my prayers answered… perhaps I rushed into things a bit too quickly? I should have been more charming… I am typically *much* more silver-tongued..." She steps toward me, slowly, inching closer and closer with every couple of words, until she's standing only a foot from me, give or take a few inches, gazing up, up, up into my eyes, her head tilted back. "But, my excitement overtook me…"

"There are literally millions of transwomen on the planet…" I mumble, lost in her eyes once more, "There's three others just across the sand, over there… what makes me so special?"

"I am not sure," she answers me, "But, I do not feel this intense attraction to any of your friends, no matter what might be between their legs. I do not feel this attraction for *any* other human—male, female, trans, or not. What I feel is for *you*, Ann, and only you. I *love* Lochlynn. I'm *in love* with her. I feel *so* much for her. The emotions are separate though—not eclipsing one another. Both can exist, no matter what Lochlynn might fear. I love her. Wholly. But, what I feel for you? It is just as powerful, just as consuming... just... separate."

"You barely know me," I whisper, "How can you know what you feel isn't just lust?"

"I've felt lust," she insists, "I've *indulged* lust. Too many times to number, if I'm honest. You absolutely inspire lust in me; but, what I feel for you is so much deeper than mere lust alone."

"I'm scared," I admit in a breathy whisper, "I don't want to love you only to lose you when you return to Atlantis. I can't make a baby with you who I will never see grow up, that I'll never get to know or love. I've lost every person I've ever loved on this planet; I can't let myself love you, just to lose you, Aegaea. And, I definitely can't create a child to love and lose. I can't. I won't."

Aegaea hesitates, stricken, torn, her face a melded medley of yearning, love, and woe. She wages some internal war behind those golden eyes. At last, she whispers, "Then, you won't. You won't *ever* lose us. I don't know how, but this I promise to you, Ann. You'll never lose me, or our daughter."

I can't stop myself as I step forward and take hold of her by the nape of her neck, pulling her toward me in a deep and passion-filled kiss.

She responds with more enthusiasm than any woman I've ever kissed before. She practically leaps into my arms, pressing her soft, subtle body to mine and knitting the fingers of both hands in my hair. Her tongue dances with mine, sweet and warm and slick.

Her hands move to my breasts and I moan as she gently caresses them, running her thumbs over my nips, taunt and erect beneath my lace bralette. She hesitates and plays with the metals bars piercing them through the center, confused.

I reach down with crossed arms and I tug my sheer blouse over my head, along with the bralette, revealing the nipple rings to her gaze.

Fascinated, she ducks her head to lick and nibble at them, tugging with her teeth until I gasp and moan and wince enough for her to show me mercy. Her palms massage and manipulate the flesh as her tongue, lips, and teeth tease.

I watch from several inches above the top of her head as her eyelashes flutter against her high cheekbones and her tongue darts between her teeth and lips to meet my flesh. I push the ringlets back from her face to get a better view.

She devours me with kisses like she's starving.

As the one who's typically the more assertive person in bed, I'm a bit taken aback by her fervor, enthusiasm, and initiative. Impressed, really...

She begins kissing a trail down my abdomen, ducking her tongue into my navel as she passes, licking all the way to where my belly disappears into my shapewear.

"Mmmm," I moan, my eyes rolling back involuntarily as I ache for more...

She hooks her fingers into the waistband of my skirt and hose and shoves them down my thighs, along with my underwear.

My organ springs forth from its fabric prison, begging for attention, for touch... for satisfaction... It throbs as it stands erect, twitching. Veins stand out from it in a pattern like rivers on a map.

It's not all that large, in truth. Many men would be self-conscious possessing something of its size; and, of course, so am I—though, for an entirely different reason. I couldn't care less about its size; its mere existence annoys me.

I look away, embarrassed by the organ that marks me 'male' to so many eyes.

A sharp, audible inhalation of breath escapes my control as Aegaea wraps her fingers around it with little warning. Her gentle but firm grasp makes my heart skip a beat and my testicles throb, heavy with the prize she so desperately desires...

She forms an 'O' with her mouth and she slips the tip inside. She flicks it gently and slowly with the tip of her tongue. Despite my aggrievance with the organ, I still enjoy the physical pleasure that her slurping and sucking brings me.

The warmth sends a shiver down my spine and I let out an unconscious, "Mmm," as I lace my fingers in her curls and pull her head toward my pelvis, shoving my cock to the back of her mouth, and just a little down her throat.

"Ngh!" She squeaks, adorably, eyes popping open and bulging slightly from the surprise. When she glances up and her eyes meet mine, though, they twinkle with humor. She giggles in the back of her throat, tickling my head...

She cups my balls in her left palm, caressing and fondling them dexterously, while she bobs her head back and forth, flattening her tongue and wrapping half-way around my shaft. Her throat creates a vacuum, sucking hard for my nectar as her fingers attempt to milk it from the source...

She nearly succeeds, too.

My cock throbs and twitches, begging to spew down her perfect throat...

I push her gently away, extracting myself from her mouth with a loud *Plop*.

Every ounce of self-control I had possessed seems to have been drained away; my body wrestles control from my mind and I find myself spinning her around and shoving her into a submissive position, on her knees and elbows, ass in the air and barely concealed by her tiny micromini sweater-dress.

The sheer hose beneath is a nonissue; I snag it intentionally with my acrylic thumbnail and I rip it open at crotch, exposing her glistening folds hugging a G-string, which I delicately pluck out of my way.

I place my finger into my own mouth a give it a good suck and lick, dampening it thoroughly, before I run it along the center fold, dipping into her opening just ever so slightly. Inside, she is slippery, warm, and *wet*.

I throb, eager with anticipation, as she moans in pleasure and desire.

Something primal, deep within my psyche, begs me for a taste... *just a little lick...*

I indulge the urge, planting my face between her lush thighs.

She tastes salty and sweet and *beachy*... I lap at her gushing breakers of ecstasy until I can battle my own desire no longer.

"My turn?" I whisper, pulling my face from her flesh and wiping the excess moister from my face with the back of my hand.

"Breed me, *please,*" Aegaea begs, lifting her ass and gleaming pussy a bit, offering it to me, "It's *meant* to be you. I can *feel it,* Ann. Please… It *has* to be *you*!"

My more carnal nature consumes me and I position myself at her entrance.

"What is this?" I wonder, mentally, *"What am I doing? Why am I doing this?"* I hadn't desired hetero-normative intercourse since I stopped trying to convince myself I needed to desire compensatory heteronormative behavior and relationships as a teenager! I am typically more of a 'power bottom'; I prefer to *receive*…

But, I am so overcome with instinct and pheromones I am like a rutting deer, driven wild with one visceral desire and need and nothing else—the drive to *breed*…

I slam my rebel cock as deep into her as my seven-and-three-quarters inches will reach, until the warm, damp flesh of her ass presses against the 'V' where my hips meet and my balls bump against her clit.

Aegaea gasps loudly, involuntarily.

I wonder, with her professed revulsion to males, if she has ever been *fucked...*

I withdraw slowly, savoring every centimeter of her rippled, shaft-hugging pussy as it squeezes me so firmly a vacuum forms and milks my very *soul* from my body, by way of my balls...

I slam back into her again, feeling my head pushing against her innermost wall.

Again, she gasps. But, this time, a weak moan also escapes her throat.

I grab her by her wide, soft hips and I pull out ever so slightly, then roll my hips forward and grind into her, deeply.

A gratifying whimper escapes her, followed by a gasp begging for more.

I find a rhythm and I rock our bodies together synchronically, caressing my head against her cervix with deep, forceful strokes.

Within minutes, her body begins to twitch in my arms and her pussy grips my dick, pulsating with wave after wave of her orgasm, pulling me deeper, attempting to *milk* my essence from me...

I won't be taken so quickly or easily, though.

I slow our stride, rocking gently back and forth, letting her ride her climax to its bitter end, and I all but pull myself from her.

She pants and her body still shakes. She glances over her shoulder, meeting my eyes and the question is evident. She suspects that we came together and our rendezvous has ended...

I can feel the grin pulling on my own lips. *'Oh-ho! Nope! You're not getting off that easy if you want* this *from me, my little mermaid...'*

I slam into her again, earning myself a small yelp of pleasure so intense it nears pain.

I squeeze both of her plush ass cheeks in my hands as I pull out and slam back in, again, guiding her hips into a new, different rocking motion.

She turns back around, hiding her face from me.

'Oh, how I wish we were somewhere with a bed, so I could flip you around and watch every wave of pleasure in your eyes...'

She is bringing out a side of me I did not even know existed; I've never felt so compelled to give a woman *whatever* she asked for as with her... She could have asked me for my left big toe and I would have given it willingly, much less a little love juice...

I grab the aquatic goddess by her shoulders and I pull her into me, grinding my hips into her bouncing butt, reaching her deepest depths and beating against her innermost door...

She opens that door for me—throws it wide open in welcome!—with another powerful orgasm, which retches from her lungs a high-pitched cry that would wake the gods.

I cannot hold back any longer.

My eyes roll back in my skull as the most powerful O I've ever achieved washes over me like a firehose. My entire frame shakes and jerks as I slump over her, attempting to bury myself even deeper as one hot stream of semen flows forth from me after another, filling her and overflowing, dripping down her trembling thighs.

A giggle escapes me as I finally extract myself from her, watching as cum flows out of her as I unplug the dam.

I'm giddy as I attempt to fix my clothing and hair and otherwise make myself presentable once more.

She does the same, a triumphant smile showing off perfect, pristinely white teeth.

She is truly one of the most beautiful women I've ever had the luck to meet...

I'm a gay transwoman—I *love* women—but, there's something about this whole encounter that doesn't sit right with me; and, as the post-coital bliss begins to wear off, I find myself sinking into a familiar state of dysphoric depression.

"D-Did you use your siren powers on me?" I whisper into the darkness, feeling the creeping sensation of paranoia on the back of my neck.

"Wh-what?!" She blinks back at me, aghast.

"Just now? To get me to fuck you? To impregnate you? Did you use your siren mind-control shit on me?" I demand, my voice louder and more firm than before. My heart races as I begin to feel taken advantage of. "Did you *magically* coerce me?"

Chapter Twelve: Sex on a Beach

Aegaea

"N-no!" I gasp, appalled and indignant, "I *swear*!" I shake my head, stepping toward her with my hands outstretched, desiring only to embrace her.

She takes a step back, away from me, "How do I know you're telling the truth? I never would have done this! I *never* would have... *created* a baby with someone I have no chance of a future with!"

"I didn't sing!" I insist, "I have to *sing* to use my powers! And, like I told you *before* our little *romp,* you *do* have a future with me, if that's what you desire! I'd give you *anything* you desire, Ann! My only desire is to be blessed to light my gaze upon you, touch you, *kiss* you, whenever the desire strikes me..."

"And, how can you do that?" she demands, "When you're miles beneath the sea?!"

Again, I step toward her, dropping my hands to take hers, enveloping them both in mine. I hold them between our hearts as I press my body to hers, gazing deep and long into her twinkling eyes.

I tap into the ancient, god-given magic that flows through my blood and I sing to her in a hushed, gentle tone, "Believe me, my love. Trust me, whitest dove. For as long as you'll have me, from the tallest mountain to the deepest sea, never will I leave your side, if only you'll say you're mine?"

She blinks back tears, her expression softening as her distrust slips away. "How?" she asks, again.

I reach up and place my palm against her cheek and she leans into my touch. "Allow me to fret the details," I instruct her in my normal, non-magical voice, "And trust that I'll *never* use my siren's voice on you without your consent. I'll *never* use it to take *any*thing from you, *especially* sex. *Especially* your genetic material. I have spent the past two decades learning how to use my voice ethically and efficiently. The effects are determined by how we *word* our song, the power lies in the notes and volume, and the duration of the effect—if not countered by a subsequent song or magic—depends on rhythm. Limits can be placed on the song's spell by adding questions at the end, as I've done. I've only given a gentle—*quiet*—nudge to help you trust and believe my words; and, if you rebuke my love, the effects end immediately."

"That's all well and good," tears roll down her cheeks, "I *do* believe you—your intentions, anyway—but *how* can you promise never to leave me, when you are sworn to become the next queen of a whole-ass nation, *underwater,* where I can never follow?!"

I smile serenely into her frantic eyes, trying my hardest to convey to her that her panic is unfounded, "Ann, Sweetest, you've made *many* misguided assumptions. Fist and foremost: I never *asked* you to follow me *anywhere*. I said *I* would follow *you*. Where we end up is, ultimately, up to you. I'd never ask you to abandon your life for me. However, if you desire a new start, arrangements could be made at Atlantis..."

"Seriously?!" Lochlynn's voice rings through the night air from behind me, making me jump and spin around to face her. She stands, arms crossed, in the shadow of the pier. Her expression is livid.

Chapter Thirteen:
I'm Not Cake!

Locklynn

"How could you?!" I scream, so enraged I can no longer control myself.

I've just witnessed with my own eyes—heard with my own ears—my whole future, my life *crumple* to pieces. If Aegaea fleas Atlantis and runs away with this human—disappears into the vast, largely unexplored surface world—and is never heard from again, my life as I know it is over, my family will be *devastated*... our kingdom will be devastated! Not to mention the emotional devastation I feel in this moment after hearing the love of my life—my *soulmate,* my best friend—profess her love for this woman she *just met*!!! That she would throw away *our life*—our kingdom—for *her*! That she would choose *her* over *me,* and all *we* held dear! That she would just *toss me aside*!!!

I cannot think rationally. I cannot forgive this.

"Lochlynn?" She breathes my name, horrified at being discovered in her emotional infidelity, "Wait… I… I love *you,* too! Obviously, the next words out of my mouth were going to be that my only stipulation be that we bring you with us…"

"Whale shit!" I snap, grinding my teeth, "You're just trying to save face! I don't trust a damn word that comes from that *cursed* mouth! The humans have a saying, you know: 'You can't have your cake and eat it, too.' It's not made much sense to me, since hear it a few weeks ago; but I get it, now. It means you can't sit something valuable aside and take it for granted and expect it to just sit there and not grow stale, collect dust, and no longer be the same delicious cake. *I'm not cake,* Aegaea! You can't have us both!"

I spin around and run—something she's still not practiced enough on her two legs to do—putting yards and yards behind me, and between her and her mistress and myself.

"No!" She wails into the clear night air, "Locklynn! *LOCKLYNN!!!*"

Chapter Fourteen:
Torn

Aegaea

As I watch Lochlynn's clownfish-colored curls bouncing down her back as she bounds away from me, my heart falls to my unsure feet.

The bond we share—the love I feel for Lochlynn—has nothing to do with Ann, though, and vice versa.

As Lochlynn disappears from my sight into the dark streets of New Orleans, I turn back to Ann. Her imploring gaze shakes me further. "I—I—I…" I stammer, glancing from Ann to the spot where Lochlynn had disappeared, and back and forth, "I *have* to go after her. *Please,* please understand…"

"I do," she says, her face softening, "You must feel really torn, right now. You need to say your piece. You should go after her. Would you rather I come with you, or give you space to deal with her… to make a decision…?"

I come up short, not comprehending, "Decision? What choice do *I* have? I cannot choose to stop loving either of you! I *am* torn—I am torn entirely in two!"

Ann steps forward and takes my hands in hers—just as I had done moments before to her—and she promises me: "She's part of you, right? Well, I accept *every* part of you. If being in your life means having her in mine…? I have seen no reason why that should be a dealbreaker, *especially* when we have this connection… when we might've just…"

"Yeah," I feel my hands on my lower stomach, imagining what might be taking place inside me, this very second… "I just with *she* could see it that way…"

"We'll *make* her see it that way," Ann promises me, placing her hands on the curve where my neck meets my shoulders and pulling me in for a deep kiss. When she pulls away, she asks me in a gentle tone, "Do you have any idea where she'd go? Any idea where we might find her?"

Chapter Fifteen: Anything but That

Lochlynn

I throw open the door to our hotel suite, meaning to grab my things and return home to my mother and sisters. I hastily begin gathering my belongings.

Within moments, though, I am shaking and bawling so furiously that I am forced to abandon my endeavor and collapse on the end of the bed, face in hands, and just *sob*.

Aegaea has slept around before—scratch that, Aegaea has never *not* slept around—but this feels different. She's never made promises to her mistresses in the past. She's only ever been her poised, haughty, image-of-regality and aloof unattainability... to everyone but me. She's never *loved* anyone but me...

I've never once doubted her devotion to me, before Ann came along...

And now, in my mind's eye, I am watching everything I hold dear crumple down around me—my past (did she *ever* truly love me?), my future... my present, *oh goddess* how the present hurts...

My chest feels as though it will implode; my blood thumps inside my veins, inside my head... Tears burn my eyes and my throat aches from the wails I fight to restrain.

"How could she just toss me aside like garbage?! How can she do this to me? Like all we are is nothing to her?! How can she just abandon me like this?"

I try to imagine my future, my life without Aegaea... and, I just *can't*. I never have before. I never would have dreamed she'd forsake me like this; she's only ever promised a future of... *us*.

And I'd give *anything* for that promised future—for her—even my own happiness, my own security.

I weep for all I've lost.

"Why couldn't I just be happy with what I had?!" I ask myself, *"Now, I've lost her... I've lost everything, all because I couldn't leave well enough alone..."*

Just then, the door to our room flies open and Aegaea stands in it.

My heart leaps in my chest at the sight of her—as it often does; perhaps it didn't get the memo...

Ann is just behind her, visible over Aegaea's much-shorter shoulder, standing in the hallway with a blank, unreadable expression plastered across her face like a mask.

"Lochlynn," Aegaea breathes my name, her eyes overflowing with anguish in the form of sparkling tears leaving trails down her round cheeks. "You have to hear me out, *please*," she begs.

I nod, wiping my tears, and she and Ann let themselves into the room. Ann closes the door behind them.

Aegaea comes to kneel on the floor before me, taking my hands into her hers and gazing deeply into my eyes. "I don't want to lose you! I *can't* lose you! You're… you're my first love; you're my best friend and my partner in everything. I can't imagine drawing breath without your love. I want the future we've always dreamed of—queens and ruling Atlantis…"

My chin trembles as I can feel my resolve vanishing.

But, then, Aegaea's expression shifts and she glances back, at Ann, and adds, "But, I never imagined meeting *anyone* like *Ann*. She… she excites me, and fulfils me in ways I didn't even know I'd been wanting, *needing,* and not finding under the ocean. She's… she's unlike anyone I've ever met. She will create Atlantis's *next* heir with me," her hand falls to her belly, in anticipation of the life that might soon fill it, "And, as such, she will *always* hold a special place in my heart, too. She wants to be part of her daughter's life and future; and, how can I fault her that? How can *you*!? You, who have lost a parent? How could you wish to deprive *our* daughter of one of hers? She *could* have three! Three amazing, loving mothers! How blessed she'd be!"

Ann steps forward and comes to sit at the foot of the bed with me, wrapping her arm around my stiff shoulders, "I don't want to be competition to you, Lochlynn," She says, "It's a contest I know I'd lose. How could I stand next to a woman as beautiful as you, who has as much history with her as you do? How could I stand a snowflake's chance in Hell? I am not into picking fights I can't win. I've never been much of a fighter, anyway. I'm more of a lover." She smiles softly at me, "I wish you'd let me show you..."

Chapter Sixteen: Honeymoon Sweet

Ann

I take a chance and I lean in, slowly, until my lips brush against Lochlynn's alabaster neck.

A sharp intake of breath and stiffening of her muscles tells me that Lochlynn still has reservations; but she does nothing to rebuke my advances. In fact, judging by the prickling of the skin up and down her arms and the salute of every tiny, translucent hair, I'd say that deep down she really, *really* wants this...

She's just scared.

And, I get it. I'd be scared to lose Aegaea, too. *I am.* She's the most amazing woman I've ever met. She's a *literal* queen. A goddess...

They both are.

I reach down and take Aegaea's hand and I pull her toward us, placing her palm against Lochlynn's firm, plump breast.

Following my lead, Aegaea locks lips with Lochlynn, leaning into her until she pushes her down, laying her across the mattress.

"Just think," Aegaea purrs, a playful smirk on her lips as she lies atop Lochlynn, their breasts smooshed together, their faces inches from one another. Aegaea massages Lochlynn's tits, cupping them from the outside with her hands, moving in slow, circular motions beneath her own. "Think about how much *fun* the *three* of us could have… Two more hands… ten more fingers… another set of lips, another tongue…" She drops her face into Lochlynn's cleavage and licks between her breasts from her collar bones to her belly.

Lochlynn shudders in anticipation for what is to come, her eyes rolling back and closing and her lips parting. A moan escapes her as Aegaea nibbles at her erect, peach-colored nipples before continuing southward.

While she pampers and pleasures Lochlynn, I set my attention on Aegaea. I am aware I have yet to earn Lochlynn's trust enough to assume so much audacity as to ask for sexual consent beyond an innocent kiss or two...

So, instead, I slip Aegaea's dress down her body and toss it aside. With similar abandon, I discard the hose I've already destroyed for her.

Briefly, I appreciate the magnificent scene before me.

Lochlynn lies on her back on the bed, spread eagle, with her tiny skirt hiked up and her flossy underwear pulled aside. The tube top she's paired with it has been tugged down, exposing her luscious boobage, which she cups with her own hands, now. Her head is thrown back in ecstasy as Aegaea buries her face between her soft thighs.

Aegaea kneels on the floor between Lochlynn's feet, functionally naked, wearing nothing more than her shoes and g-string. Her breasts are full and teardrop-shaped as they dangle, unoccupied.

To remedy that situation, I kneel behind her and grab handfuls of her tits, squeezing and massaging.

Aegaea moans into Lochlynn's wisps of orange fur in pleasure, lapping at the glistening, gleaming pink flesh below.

I can feel myself twitching and throbbing as blood is redirected and begins to fill the most sensitive part of my body. It *aches* for the warm, soft, *wet* folds it just tasted less than an hour ago...

Greedy, greedy, greedy...

In an act of self-denial and self-discipline, I refuse the urge and instead lower my face to meet her raised ass, releasing my double grips on her breasts and grabbing her ass cheeks, spreading them. Before my eyes, her dark skin glistens.

Her soft, salty musk reaches my nose and my erection throbs even more insistently; but, again, I ignore it and focus on the beautiful vagina spread before me, waiting and begging to be devoured...

To the very last drop...

I lean in and my lips part, allowing my tongue to escape. I taste her now-familiar flavor, deeply inhaling her scent as my tongue stretches to reach the small, hard knot just past her opening.

When I find the elusive, hidden gem, I tease it relentlessly with the tip of my tongue, darting and flicking. I trace circles around it, sucking on it occasionally, pulling it between my lips.

Aegaea gasps and moans into Lochlynn's pussy as she pumps her arm back and forth, using three fingers of her right hand to fuck Lochlynn's pink slit while the thumb of the left hand teases her rear entrance.

Lochlynn's thighs tremble and jerk as she is overcome in a violent orgasm. She arches her back and cries out, eyes rolling in her head and mouth agape.

Aegaea slips another finger into her as the orgasm wanes and her muscles relax. It slides in easily and, as soon as it disappears inside, Aegaea adds her thumb, as well, pumping her fist in and out, in and out...

Mimicking the way she makes love to Lochlynn, I add another finger to Aegaea's dripping pussy. Three, total.

Then, another: four.

And, the thumb.

With immense satisfaction, my entire fist disappears into her warm depths and I fuck her with it, stretching and pounding her to an extreme my much-smaller dick could never achieve.

Aegaea yowls like a cat in heat as she clamps down on my hand and I feel the orgasm roll through the walls of her cunt, pulling my fingers deeper with surprising strength.

Inside, I massage her cervix with the tips of my three longest fingers, feeling the creamy fluids accumulating.

As my right hand and fingers play with her inner-most pleasure zone, my left tweaks and twiddles her clit. I alternate circular movements with back-and-forth flicking, throwing in a light pinch here and there.

While my hands work tirelessly—gratefully slaving away for my queens—I am sure to put my best feature to good use, as well.

I pucker up and I tenderly kiss the pucker she presents right before my face. My lips move against the delicate, sensitive flesh, pulling inward with each smooch. My tongue darts in and out, teasing the wrinkled, clenching sphincter as it denies my entrance with reluctance.

I grin into her asscheeks as I flex the muscle I work out more regularly—and with much more passion—than any other in my body. I press the tip into her bootyhole, moving it in slow, circular movements to help loosen the hesitant outlet.

Aegaea squeaks apprehensively—adorably—and forgets her activities with Lochlynn's bits for a moment, gasping as my tongue penetrates her rectum over and over, and over.

I do not neglect my hand's tasks, though—I'm quite the multitasker—and I continue to pound her pussy with the fist of my right hand, while my left rubs furiously, flat-fingered, against her sopping-wet clit and lips.

Within just a few heartbeats, Aegaea cries out and sprays my arm and face, squirting her sweet nectar in wave after wave of intense orgasm.

She collapses on top of Lochlynn, trembling, giggling, exhausted and unable to think at all. Her eyes close and the two share a deep, passionate kiss.

Knowing this is the optimal opportunity to breed her, I grab Aegaea by the hips and position myself behind her.

I am fully erect, throbbing, and leaking pre-cum as I align the head with her entrance.

"Ohhh," Aegaea moans, her eyes flying open, as she feels me. "Wai—" she gasps, uncertain of her own capacity for pleasure.

But, she speaks too late and I have already slammed my cock balls-deep into her. She gasps sharply.

I hesitate, "Wait?" I ask, pausing with my dick buried in her, "Do you really mean that? Do you want me to stop?" A grin plays at my lips because I already know her answer.

She pants, "N-no, *please*, keep going... *fill me*..."

I need no other encouragement.

I slide myself out, nearly withdrawing completely, and then I yank her ass toward me, delving deep as her very soul, yet again.

She yelps, then moans, her eyes rolling back.

Lochlynn, spent of her own pleasure for the moment, reaches down with her right hand to slowly, tenderly caress her clit, just above where my dick slides in and out, in and out. With her left hand, she plays with Aegaea's right breast—pinching and lightly twisting her nipples, tugging on them to a degree that must edge on pain...

Aegaea moans in what can only be pleasure, though, and *a lot* of pleasure, at that.

Holding her hips like handles, I rock back and forth, grinding the head of my dick against her cervix.

With my thumb, I play with her booty, knowing the sensation will add a tantalizing distraction from all the other pleasure overwhelming her brain.

Aegaea gasps, panting, her frantic hands grabbing Lochlynn's breasts as she buries her face between them to scream out her next climax.

The rippling spasms of her inner walls pull me deeper in, working to milk me for all I'm worth. I cannot control myself, cannot hold back the flood of sperm that explodes from me, filling her womb for a second time tonight...

Chapter Seventeen: Land Ho

Aegaea

The early morning sun cascades through the large, pristinely clear windows, dancing across our faces and bodies. I come to slowly, reluctantly, clinging to the remaining few moments of warm, snuggly bliss that exists within this landscape of white blankets and smooth, multi-hued, naked skin.

I'm not sure, at first, what has dragged me from my *very* pleasant slumber and dream; however, by the time the next timid tap at the door reaches my ears, I remember.

Frowning, I roll over and bury my face deeper into the sweet-smelling fabrics. "*I never want to leave this spot...*" I think to myself, lamenting the tragedy of cutting short our cuddle-session. "*Maybe, if I ignore whoever it is, they'll just go away and leave us alone...?*"

Such is too much to hope for, though, and a third knock follows, louder than the first two. And, a voice: "Your Majesty? Commander? Hello?" It's Orvius, of course.

I sigh and groan, throwing the closest pillow over my head, "GO AWAY!" I growl, loudly.

On either side of me, Ann and Lochlynn stir, waking from their peaceful slumbers.

"Your Majesty," Yandra's voice joins Orvius's, louder, "We must request an audience. Regarding last night's... *unaccompanied excursion?*"

I sigh and roll over so that I can scoot to the bottom of the bed without disturbing my lovers any more than necessary. I grab the white silk robe hanging next to the door to cover my bare naked body, and I fling open the door. "Never mind my unsanctioned expedition," I brush off their concerns with a flippant wave of my hand, vaguely gesturing to the two women sleeping naked in my bed. Ann's sleepy salute raising both sets of brows. "As you can see, we made it safely back.

Our mission topside has been accomplished and transportation back to Atlantis shall be chartered for the *five* of us, immediately."

"Five?!" Yandra gasps, glancing again to the bed, "The human? It's unheard of! Forbidden!"

"And *I,* as the next queen, am the one to declare what is forbidden and outlawed and what is *not,* and I declare Ann shall return with us."

"How?" Yandra's voice rings in perfect harmony with Ann's behind us, from the bed.

I glance over my shoulder to see her sitting up, now, clutching the blankets around herself, face flush. Lochlynn sits next to her, red-faced and wide-eyed, abashed.

I turn around and smile fondly upon the beautiful sight that is both of my lovers sharing this bed, wrapped in pristine white sheets. I feel no shame, no guilt, no reservations. I *will* feel no such thing, ever. Not for something so perfectly beautiful. I am *proud* of the family we are creating.

"If you will accept the offer, that is?" I ask, holding my breath.

Ann pauses for just a moment, before a huge smile spreads across her face, "Of course! I'd *love* to go home with you to Atlantis! But, how can that be possible?"

I turn my attention to Lochlynn, pleading with my eyes, "Lochlynn could, theoretically, change *you* into the form of a mermaid with just as much ease as she changed me into this 'human' one. *If* she will? If she'll do this, for me?"

My request is met with stone-faced silence—a long one. Lochlynn's green eyes lock with mine and refuse to relinquish their intense hold. It's as though she's searching for something within me.

Finally, she relents and speaks; barely above a whisper, she asks, "What will that mean for you and I?"

"That we have one more parent to care for this baby," I tell her, "That we have one more body to keep us warm in bed at night. That we have one more mind to help rule."

“Would she be Queen Consort, or I?”

I chew this over. I do not want to start our newfound family off on the wrong precedent. While I know Ann would not covet or resent the position, now, I am not so sure that will be the case a few years down the road. Yet, I do not wish to place Ann’s possible future desires over Lochlynn’s current *needs*. And, in this moment, Lochlynn needs reassurance.

“I would like to think,” I begin, slowly, “That possibly, one day in the future, *both* of you could hold the honor and power of the position as Queen Consort. I see no reason Atlantis would suffer from having *three* rulers, rather than two; in fact, I can only see how this arrangement would *benefit* our kingdom.” I glance back at Orvius and Yandra’s flabbergast faces. “Of course, I will have to run this notion past my mother and the Council of Queens. However, initially, immediately upon our return to Lumeria Palace, I would like to take *you* as my Queen Consort, in order to solidify and sanctify our union and your station. I would have liked to have been given the chance to ask you to become my wife in a more romantic, theatrical manner, though..."

Tears spill forth from Lochlynn's eyes and an emotional smile pulls at her trembling lips, "Really?" she peeps, "You're not just saying these things to placate me?"

"Of course not," I assure her, "It has always been my plan to ask for your hand in marriage upon our return from the surface, Lochlynn. Have we not had many, extensive conversations to the effect, before this expedition? Like I have said, multiple times, my feelings for Ann have absolutely no impact on my emotions for or plans I've made with you. As queen, am I not expected to show love and familiarity with an entire kingdom of citizens? Why should I not be allowed to receive the love of but one? Why am I allowed but one person to lean upon, when an entire nation leans upon me?!"

Chapter Eighteen: Wildest Dreams

Ann

The reality of visiting the lost city of Atlantis seems impossible, fantastical. I can barely wrap my head around the future Aegaea proposes.

Would I miss New Orleans, my friends, America and the surface world at large? If I'm honest? When compared with the possibility of a future as a mermaid with Aegaea and Lochlynn, miles beneath the waves, living in the near-utopic paradise that Aegaea describes as Atlantis?

Not particularly.

What's to miss? Homophobia? Transphobia? Religious bigotry? Capitalism and taxes? Forty-to-eight-hour work weeks? Grinding out an existence by tolerating gropey, misogynistic, disgusting men?

Pollution and climate change?

The likely apocalypse baring down on humanity as a result of our carelessness?

Nope.

My family disowned me, years ago. Even my closest friends are relationships of convenience and trauma-bonds.

There's *literally* nothing and no one holding me here. At least none that I'd place above Aegaea.

Aegaea's male security officer accompanies she and I to my apartment to grab the few sentimental items I have enough of an attachment to that I might regret abandoning. Meanwhile, Lochlynn and the security officer named 'Yandra' remain in their suite to contact the coordinator of transportation in something called 'Orbs'.

Within less than two hours, we are packed and taking a Uber to a remote, undisclosed location.

After a lengthy ride, the driver pulls off the main road and pulls alongside a sandbank off the river, near where it dumps into the Gulf of Mexico.

We all clamber out of the black economy minivan and retrieve our bags from the hatchback. With little in way of parting niceties, the Uber Driver pulls off, seemingly not even bothered by having dropped off five strangers—four women and a man—in the middle of ButtFuck nowhere. As if this doesn't all scream "Human Trafficking" when taken out of context...

But, as soon as the minivan is out of sight, a large bubble-like pod emerges from the murky, muddy waters, beaching itself in the sand. The vehicle seems to be unmanned, and just large enough for the five of us to squeeze inside and sit knee-to-knee.

Once inside, the clear dome encapsulates us and the pod retreats from the shore, diving deeper and deeper, skimming along the silty, muddy bed of the great Mississippi.

After a stretch of time, the water clears—with what seem to be unnatural swiftness—of its rivery murkiness and becomes remarkably crystal clear. The brown-ish gray silt morphs into white sand and shells.

Eventually, the light fades, filtered by so many hundreds of feet of ocean water, and we travel in complete darkness for what feels like an endless forever.

When the darkness wanes, though, the glorious city that slowly appears and grows closer and closer is utterly breathtaking. A bubble like the one we ride in—but a million times larger—encloses a city at least as large as New Orleans, perhaps larger. Light emanates from the city, blue-ish white. The architecture seems to be largely influenced by coral and other similar lifeforms that exist on the ocean floor, though scaled up by several hundred thousand, or million.

Every surface seems to sparkle, as though glitter is mixed into the concrete that goes into the structures, the roadways, the statues… It's like a glam wet dream.

I'm instantly in love.

Our bubble-car floats downward, and downward, until it reaches the bubble-dome surrounding the city.

I assume, at first, that inside the dome is air. I was wrong, though.

As the otherworldly vehicle makes contact with the dome, it seems to absorb us, like one soap bubble merging with another.

The bubble-car reemerges on the other side of the bubble-dome, floating on what is very much water...

I begin to panic. When this aquatic UFO opens, am I going to drown?!

As we near the largest structure within sight of the city now spanning watery horizon to water horizon—what is obviously the gorgeous Lumeria Palace mentioned by Aegaea and Lochlynn—I can see mermaids—*actual fucking mermaids!!!*—swimming around, majestically.

Among the mermaids, I also notice similar beings, some wearing pelts of various oceanic mammals, some are nearly completely transformed into those animals, and a few of what would normally appear to just *be* the otters, seals, dolphins, walruses, etc., aside from the tasks they perform and the obvious conversations they hold with the mermaids.

Selks.

And, among the mermaids and selkies, a few ethereal beings in floaty, wispy fabrics, with shells and jewels and strange coral-like growths growing from their bodies.

Sylphs.

The Bubble descends upon a courtyard in the center of the castle and comes to rest upon the glistening marble-like ground.

I glance around the bubble, hoping I'm not the only one who hasn't forgotten my inability to breathe down here.

Aegaea and Lochlynn both smile at me, and I relax, knowing they have not forgotten me or my needs.

"Are you ready?" Aegaea asks me, leaning across the bubble to take my hands, "It doesn't hurt; I swear on my life."

"There's just one thing," Lochlynn says, her face hesitant, "There's no *male* mermaids. I wouldn't even *know* how to… I have to *visualize* your new form, you know?"

"So," I glance between her and Aegaea, not able to believe what I'm hearing, "So, I'll be… I'll be a girl. Like, *anatomically*? Completely?"

"Yes," she says, her eyes gauging my reaction, "Perhaps I should have mentioned this while we were still on the surface?"

Tears roll down my face as I blink them away. I wipe them carefully, not wanting to smudge what's left of my makeup.

"Are you alright?" Aegaea asks, concern evident in her voice.

"Y-Yes," I stammer, "This is… this is, like, my *wildest* dream come true…"

A radiant smile spreads across Aegaea's face. She leans across the bubble and kisses me, deeply.

When we lean away from one another, Lochlynn grabs ahold of me by my neck and yanks me to her, planting a deep kiss on me, too.

When our lips part, the bubble around us pops, water instantly fills the space around us, slapping against my face.

Fear consumes me for just a moment. I hold my breath. But, then, I glance down and I see that, from the hips down, my legs have been replaced with silvery-white scales and a tail that ends in the most glorious, translucent fin.

We are in Atlantis.

And, I am a mermaid.

Chapter Nineteen: Queen Mother

Lochlynn

Aegaea is a vision in gold as she holds her chin high in regal, royal pride, her face stoic and respectably reserved as her mother places the tall crown upon her brow.

The former Queen turns, slowly, to face me. As she flats before me, holding a slightly-smaller crown out, placing it upon my lowered head, a tear glistens in the corner of her eye.

Together, Aegaea and I turn to face the honored guests of our marriage and coronation ceremony.

Ann beams at us from the front row, overjoyed and filled with pride.

As Aegaea and I bow to our public, greeting them—for the first time—as the ruling couple, she places the hand not clutching mine atop her round bell.

She positively glows.

The End

FOR EXCLUSIVE CONTENT, visit:

Cskellyofficial.wordpress.com/erotic-fantasy

- Official Soundtrack
- Character Profiles and Artwork
- Illustration
- Links to other works by Kelly Comans (Erotica); aka: C.S. Kelly (Non-erotic fiction) & K. Boutwell (Nonfiction)

www.ingramcontent.com/pod-product-compliance
Lightning Source LLC
LaVergne TN
LVHW050545160826
845677LV00011B/2179

* 9 7 9 8 3 7 3 8 7 0 6 6 5 *